One

Saturday

Evening

T.K. Chapin

One SATURDAY EVENING

T.K. CHAPIN

Best selling author of "Amongst the Flames"

One Saturday Evening

DEDICATION

Dedicated to my loving wife.

For all the years she has put up with me

And many more to come.

CONTENTS

ACKNOWLEDGMENTS

First and foremost, I want to thank God. God's salvation through the death, burial and resurrection of Jesus Christ gives us all the ability to have a personal relationship with the creator of the Universe.

I also want to thank my wife. She's my muse and my inspiration. A wonderful wife, an amazing mother and the best person I have ever met. She's great and has always stood by me with every decision I have made along life's way.

I'd like to thank my editors and early readers for helping me along the way. I also want to thank all of my friends and extended family for the support. It's a true blessing to have every person I know in my life.

AUTHOR'S NOTE

Thank you for choosing to read **One Saturday Evening**. I wrote this book to help people that are going through difficulties in their life. Oftentimes it's not until we stop trying that God can truly begin to work in our lives. The story centers on a woman that has been divorced, but I find her pain and trials in life are easily identifiable. My hope for this story is that it blesses you as much as it did me writing it.

And we know that in all things God works for the good of those who love him, who have been called according to his purpose.

Romans 8:28

PROLOGUE

When I uttered those sweet words, 'I do,' I thought it would be forever. My forever only turned out to be sixteen years. That's life though. It's full of the unexpected. Right when you think you have a handle on things, something disastrous happens, like your husband leaving you one day for no apparent reason. Why'd Bradley leave? I don't know. Maybe it was the three children we had and the toll it took on my body, or maybe he just got bored with me. I don't like thinking it was because of either of those two things, but he left, no matter the reason.

He left me with an 'I don't' and three souls to take care of by my lonesome self. With Bradley gone, along with his income, I was forced to move back to my hometown of Newport. That was two years ago now. It's by no means perfect here, but the town and air have a flavor that reminds me of my childhood days roaming the streets and playing with friends, and I like that feeling.

CHAPTER 1

Though I had come to terms with being alone, my heart longed to be loved. The morning cups of coffee and Bible reading were truly my greatest joy in life, but in the back of my mind, I knew just how sweet the mornings were with a husband by my side. My heart had been conditioned for too long to know what it felt like to always have someone there for me—whenever I woke up, whenever I came home, and most painful of all . . . whenever I pillowed my head to sleep at night. Now, even two years later, my heart still has a longing for the companionship and love. I never dreamed I'd be in the situation I found myself in.

Everything changed without my even knowing it on the last day of school for my three daughters. I was sitting in my kitchen one early morning, reading my Bible and taking sips of my coffee with a dash of hazelnut creamer, when I suddenly heard the sound of a truck backing up outside. Curious, I left my Bible and cup of coffee on the kitchen table to go investigate.

Opening the front door, I peeked out and spotted a moving truck next door at Mr. Finley's old place. Mr. Finley had been a local resident of Newport from as far back as I could remember into my childhood, but he had died a few summers before I moved back to town with the girls. His once large and vibrant four-story house stood on a beautiful and well-kept acre and a half just off Diamond Lake. It now stood vacant, with overgrowth and a slouching roof on one end. My mother had told me when I asked about the property that the children didn't want to sell it, but they felt it was better left alone. It piqued my interest, to say the least, to see a moving truck over there.

"Mom?" a familiar voice startled me from behind, breaking me out of my thoughts.

"Yes, dear?" I asked, whipping around to see Emily, my sixteen-year-old, tilting her head as she looked at me from atop the stairs.

"Have you seen my lip gloss?"

I shook my head and stole one more glance out the door toward Mr. Finley's. I saw a man this time. He was coming around the back of the moving truck. He looked about my age, and though the distance was great between my front door and him, I could tell he was attractive. *Probably married.* Closing the door and my thoughts, I turned around and went

7

upstairs to help Emily find her lip gloss.

As Emily, along with Tristan, my ten-year-old, and Bailey, my seven-year-old, piled into the SUV that morning, I noticed the brown-haired mystery man coming out of the back of the moving truck with a couple of boxes stacked in his arms. Two more men were there now, but they were still in the truck. Squinting, I could see they were positioning an old baby grand piano onto rollers. A warmth of love from my past rushed over me at the sight of the piano. It reminded me of the piano my grandfather would play when I was a child when all our family would gather for the holidays. Those days were some of the best memories I had in my life. The world made sense back when I was a child, but I didn't know it did until I grew too old to appreciate it.

"Mom!" Emily startled me out of my reminiscent state as I stood at the driver side door staring at the moving truck. Shaking it off, I climbed into the driver's seat and made eye contact with my beloved, but bossy, daughter in the rearview mirror.

"Yes, Emily?"

"I can't be late. I have to turn in that extra credit to Mrs. Platt." Her eyes drifted over to Mr. Finley's house and the moving truck I was looking at only moments earlier. "Who's moving in next door?"

"I'm not sure." My eyes found their way back over to see the piano rolling down the ramp. Who was this new mysterious guy who'd moved in next door? I wasn't sure, but I planned to find out.

As I backed out of my driveway, I pulled my thoughts away from the mysterious new arrival to the neighborhood and focused on the day ahead. Dropping the kids off at school for their last day, I stopped by the grocery store for a few needed items, and then headed off to my shift at Dixie's Diner.

Click.

She hung up. Glancing at my phone for a moment, I shook my head and set it down on the counter nearby. Edith didn't know what she was talking about. I knew Dylan now. He was a good man and a man of God. The water finished heating for my tea, and I went over to pour myself a cup along with a cup of coffee for Dylan.

Coming out to the patio, I handed Dylan his cup and sat down next to him, setting my cup down on the patio table between our chairs. Relaxing with a cup of tea in front of the fire with him was the perfect end to a perfect day. Feeling his eyes on me, I turned to him. "What is it?" I asked.

He took a drink and set it down. "Today was awesome. I haven't been able to have fun like that in so long."

"I agree. It was a blast, and the girls loved it too."

He leaned over the table separating us and used his index finger to gently guide my chin and head over to him. He leaned in and slowly kissed me as the fire let out a loud pop. As our lips touched and the warmth of his love came over me, I felt every part of my body begin to melt into him. I hesitated for a moment to relax, and then all my walls came tumbling down. Losing control over all my senses, I reached up with my hands gently touching his face. The light stubble of his facial hair grazed my skin. His hand came up and laid claim to my hair. His touch, his lips, his everything was intoxicating and I wanted more.

Climbing out of my chair and across the patio table,

I kicked over our cups as I landed into his arms and lap. Pulling back gently from our kiss, he asked, "Our cups?"

"I don't care." Quickly, I dipped back into kissing him as the yearning for more came over me. Each kiss felt as if it were pulling me further into him and made me want more. His hands ran up and down my back, into my hair, and then caressing my arms. I didn't want him to ever stop. Those hands—they were the rough and rugged hands of a man who worked hard, yet he was able to touch me with such tenderness and gentleness. His fingers soon ran back along my neckline and down my arm, sending waves of chills and desire through my body.

Another pop came from the fire and we both glanced over. It was roaring fiercely, but it paled in comparison to the heat we had between us in the moment. Our eyes met, and I saw through him and into his soul. He didn't speak a word, but I saw it— love. Dipping my lips to his, I began to kiss him more.

Suddenly, Dylan stopped and gently pushed me back and off his lap. He smiled and leaned to the front of his chair. Brushing a piece of hair behind my ear, he let his palm press against my cheek. I let my cheek lay against his palm.

"What are you doing?" I asked with a bit of agitation.

Looking into my eyes, he said, "I care about you. I think it's best that I go."

Leaning in, he kissed me softly on the lips, driving my desire deeper.

"Please stay a while longer." My eyes begged and my

heart pleaded.

"That's not the right thing to do here, Charlotte. We both know that." He took my hand in both of his and kissed my palm, folding my fingers to caress the lingering memory. Standing, he headed back to his house. As I watched him walk away, the fire within me that wanted that man grew tenfold. He was truly a man of God. He knew if he would've pushed, I would have given in, and he didn't let that happen. Letting the fire smolder both in the fireplace and within me, I turned in for the evening.

CHAPTER 13

The following day after church, my mother and Dylan came over to my house for lunch. After turkey sandwiches, the girls and Dylan went out in the backyard to play a game of croquet. Sitting down on the patio with my mother and our glasses of iced tea, I looked out into the yard. Seeing Dylan play, laugh and goof around with the girls brought a smile to my face.

"You like him."

Turning to my mother, I looked down and shook my head. "*Mom.*"

"You do." Her eyes followed Dylan in the yard as she nodded slowly. "I can see why . . . he's so good with the girls, kind-hearted, handsome, and most

CHAPTER 2

After helping with dishes all morning after a big breakfast rush, I was more than ready for my lunch break. As I sat down with my chef salad in a booth, Miley came over and sat down with me.

"You want to get together tonight? I need a girl's night. How about you?"

I smiled. "I don't know. I'm little on the tired side."

"You okay? You seemed a little lost in thought all morning in the back."

Finishing my bite of salad, I nodded. "I'm fine. Just thinking about the new neighbor who moved in next door."

"Thinking about the neighbor?"

"Yeah. He's cute." My thoughts drifted back in time to earlier that day when I saw him.

"Single?"

"I don't know . . . probably not."

Miley let out a laugh and reached across the table, grasping my free hand. "Don't think that way. He could be. You never know . . . you know?"

"Yeah. I suppose you're right, but I have three kids and I'm pretty sure I'm older than him. He probably doesn't want all this baggage if he is free."

Miley looked me in the eyes. "You have a lot to offer, Charlotte. You have a big heart and can cook like nobody I've ever met! Don't tell Serenah that though."

I laughed. "Thanks." As I sat and finished my salad,

my mind began to wander to the new neighbor. I pictured us walking along the shore with the sun setting across the lake, drinking a cup of coffee together at my kitchen table, and even sharing a cup of tea under the stars on my back porch. Realizing I was daydreaming about a complete stranger, I snapped myself out of it and headed back for the rest of my shift.

I spent the second half of my shift helping bus tables and serving until around four thirty, when two of the vilest people walked in—the Atkin brothers, Frank and Cody. The Townson family's enemy was the Atkins family. And while I wasn't a Townson by blood, I did find myself aligned with their family. In my youth, I had taken piano lessons from Edith Townson. She might be quite a bit older than me, but she was one of my closest friends I had in Newport.

Slipping to the back of the restaurant as my heart pounded, I hoped to avoid waiting on their table. I watched from the small window in the swinging doors. Feeling my anger rise inside me, I asked out loud, "Why? Why must the lousy Atkin brothers come here?"

A snicker came from behind me and I turned around. It was the cook Diego. He was logging into the computer for his shift.

"It's not funny." I turned back to look through the little window and back at the table the brothers were sitting at. "I can't stand the Atkin's family."

"You'll have to take their table. Wendy is sending Miley home early."

"Ugh. *Fine.*" There was nothing I could do to get out of it. With a fake smile, I pushed open the swinging doors and headed toward their table. Every step I got closer, I prayed for God's help. It'd be a miracle if I could get through taking their order without slapping one of them across the face. There was too much history. Arriving at their table, I forced my fake smile wider and pulled out my pen and pad to take their order. Faking happiness wasn't too hard for me. I had been accustomed to it as a server for two years now. There seemed to always be a few— let's say . . . *inconvenient*—customers almost weekly. "What can I get for you, gentlemen? I mean, guys?"

"Rude." Frank crossed his arms on the table and leaned in to laugh a little. Then he looked up at me. "What about some food?"

"Okay." *I can't do this. They're just going to be immature.* Dropping my hand to my side, I began to walk away.

"Come back! I'm just playing." Frank motioned me back to the table with a wave and a smile.

I kept my composure and headed back to their table. I sent another prayer up. I needed God's ability to show grace and mercy. There was too much anger and anxiety built up over all that was going on between the Townson and the Atkin families. My self-control petered out and my self-will took hold. "Are you ready to order, Mr. Atkin?" My eyes shifted to another customer's table in the restaurant. "Or would you rather just steal someone else's plate of food?"

His smile turned into a tight-lipped expression. His voice deepened. "We're going to find *our* bell and there's not a thing you or that Townson family can do about it. We have family from all across the country showing up to Newport to finally retrieve our bell from Diamond Lake."

Smirking, I said, "We'll see about that."

"We're closing in on the bell. I can *feel* it," Cody added.

"Oh, yeah?" Raising an eyebrow, I continued. "You have a lead?"

Frank shook his head. "Don't worry about it. You just worry about our food getting to us hot. We'll take two cokes and a couple chicken clubs, Ms.

Charlotte."

They didn't have any leads. They were probably just jerking me around, but it drove me nuts regardless. My cheeks began to burn from trying to keep the fake smile on my face as I went to the back of the restaurant. As the swinging doors closed, I exploded. "Those self-righteous Atkin brothers are so agitating!" I ripped the order from my pad and tossed it up on the order rack.

"Jeez," Diego said as he glanced around the corner of the metal shelves he was at further in the back.

Walking back to him as he pulled down the box of napkins from a top shelf, I continued. "They're jerks, Diego. I can't stand them! I'm not even a Townson, but I just don't like them!"

Diego kept quiet as he opened the box of napkins.

"I'm sure they're wonderful people in their circles of friends and family, but I cannot stand their rudeness toward anyone who doesn't agree with them."

"Aren't *you* rude toward the Atkins?" he asked.

"No . . . maybe. I don't know. I try to be nice." My mind wandered. Was Frank telling the truth about having family coming to town to help expand the search of the Townson's lost bell? What if it was true? I needed to tell the Townsons what I learned, regardless of it being true or not. It could help them speed up their own efforts. "I'm taking a break." Undoing my apron from my waist, I tossed it onto the nearby counter and headed through the back door.

Moments later Wendy came outside. "You on break?" she asked snidely.

"Yeah. Sorry."

"Let someone other than the cook know next time," she retorted and went back inside.

Shaking my head as I walked away I called Edith.

"*Charlotte.*" Edith answered with an elegant tone that conveyed both gentleness and joy to hear from me. "To what do I owe this pleasure?"

"Hey, Edith." Glancing through a side window into the restaurant, my eyes fell on Frank and Cody. "Do you know about the Atkins having family come to town?"

"There is a rumor floating around about an Atkin cousin purchasing *The Newport Theater.*"

Pressing my hand against my forehead, I turned and began to pace. "Really?"

"Yes, but why do you ask, dear?"

"A couple of Atkin brothers came into the diner and were talking about closing in on your family's bell in the lake."

"Interesting . . ." Her tone shifted to concern, and then she paused for a moment before continuing. "Keep your eyes and ears open, Charlotte. Would you?"

"I'll let you know anything I find out, Edith." As I hung up the phone, I saw Frank purposely knock over his cup of soda onto the floor, and then he and Cody began to laugh.

Returning back inside after my phone call with Edith, I felt my annoyance with the Atkin family rising. Like a summer storm moving in, I was ready to dart back into the dining room and smack Frank upside the head for the stunt he pulled. How dare he come into my place of work and show such a lack of respect? He had no right. Cutting through the kitchen, I grabbed my server apron and went through the swinging doors back into the restaurant.

They were gone.

Glancing at Miley over at the register, I asked, "Where'd they go?"

"They paid and changed the order to be a 'to-go' and left when it was done. Just a minute ago."

"Surprise they actually paid for their meal. Last time they left they just told Miley I offered to buy their meal." Glancing toward the parking lot, my kindling wrath began to dwindle as relief took over that they were gone.

After stopping by my mother's house to pick up the girls, I arrived back home to spot the mysterious new neighbor sitting out on the back of the moving truck. His help seemed to have left and he looked a bit lonely. I wondered if perhaps his wife was out gathering new cleaning supplies for the house. I had always done that each time Bradley and I moved somewhere new. Regardless, I felt it was proper to go introduce myself and welcome him and his family to the neighborhood.

"Go ahead inside," I told the girls as we got out of the car. They headed toward the house while I crossed the patch of grass that separated our properties. He didn't see me on my approach, but I kept my eyes on him. He was attractive, but I dismissed any desire that I felt in the moment. A man who looked like that *had* to be taken.

"Hey," I said with a grin as I approached him.

He jumped a little and spilled his glass of lemonade on his shirt. "Hey . . ."

"I'm so sorry! I didn't mean to startle you. I'm your neighbor—Charlotte."

"It's okay. I'm Dylan." He extended a hand to shake mine as he set his lemonade down beside him. My wandering eyes couldn't help but notice there was no ring on his finger. *Not married? Or just the type of guy who doesn't wear a ring? Hmm . . .* His arms were well defined and his white tee shirt was tight against his body in all the right places. It was difficult to not let my mind wander too long as I looked him over. Turning my head, I glanced over at the house.

"So you're the brave soul that took on the abandoned house? When I took a peek inside a couple of years back, it was pretty bad in there."

"It just needs some love." He stood up and stood closer to me as he pointed to the front steps. "You see that overgrowth out front? It'd take less than an afternoon to clean up."

He might have been moving all day, but I got a whiff of his scent and it was heavenly. I needed to know if he was married quickly. "Is that factoring in help from your . . . wife?"

He shook his head and sat back down on the end of the truck. "No wife. Just me."

Dylan gazed back over at the house. "Shouldn't take

more than a week to clean up and get the electrical fixed in the house. I can 'rough it' until then." Our eyes connected as he finished his sentence.

Warmth washed over me as I looked into his golden brown eyes. He was handsome, and that fact terrified me. "Neat." My eyes turned back to the house. "I'm sure if Mr. Finley were still alive, he would have been happy to see someone move in and fix it up."

He raised an eyebrow. "Who's that?"

"He used to live here. He was an old guy who lived in this house clear back to when I was a kid. That was a long time ago, and the house was old then!" Letting out a bit of a laugh, I said, "Guess I'm dating myself with that comment."

He laughed. "I wouldn't guess you're over twenty-five."

I blushed. This guy is laying on the charm big time, and before he even gets moved into his house. Smiling, I shook my head. "Try thirty-seven."

His eyebrows shot up as he leaned forward. "No way! I couldn't have guessed that in a million years."

"How old are you, Dylan?"

"I'm thirty-eight." He stood up and touched the side of my arm. "Come in and let's get you a glass of lemonade."

Stepping back, I shook my head. "I can't. I gotta get back to my girls."

He raised an eyebrow. "I'm sorry. I didn't even think to ask. Are you married?"

"I'm *very* single. I just need to get them some

dinner."

"Ah . . . I gotcha."

Our eyes connected and we both smiled. The slight awkwardness I felt in the moment reminded me I hadn't dated much since Bradley. I tried online dating, but it didn't work out at all. The only guys I could manage to find always ended up weird, and most were downright creepy. The best date I was able to muster up from online dating was dinner and a movie, but all he did was talk the entire way through the movie. He gabbed on and on about how corrupt Hollywood had become over the years and how they're a working hand of Satan.

Interrupting our moment, a faint but very distinct voice called out to me. Turning my head, I saw it was Bailey hollering from the doorway and waving me over. Looking back at Dylan with a smile, I said, "I'd better get going."

"It was nice meeting you, Charlotte." He extended his hand again. Just to feel the touch of him, even for a moment, brought a certain comfort to me.

My smile grew as I tilted my head. "It was nice meeting you too." As I crossed the grass, I glanced back to catch him still looking at me.

"Feel free to come by anytime," he said.

I smiled and kept walking back to my house. He was cute, charming, and not married. Life just got a little more interesting.

CHAPTER 3

After dinner, I baked a dozen chocolate chip cookies for the girls to take over to Dylan. In the Gilroy family, we had a longstanding tradition of welcoming newcomers to the neighborhood with sweets. I remember as a child my mother hustling to the kitchen at the first sighting of a moving truck pulling into the neighborhood. Oftentimes, it'd be a plate of cookies or brownies, but on occasion, she'd make her famous four-layer dessert. My sister, Abby, and I were always tasked, once we were old enough, to take the freshly baked goods to the newcomers.

As I wrapped the plate of cookies with tinfoil, I called for the girls to come downstairs to the kitchen. As they came down the stairs and through the living room, I could hear the girls exchanging giggles.

"Those smell *so* good, Mom!" Tristan said.

"They're for our new neighbor next door, Dylan. I want you girls to take them to him." I gave Emily the plate of cookies. She sighed heavily.

"I'm not a kid anymore," Emily blurted out. "This is a *kid* thing to do."

"Lead by example and by listening, please." Glancing toward the back door and then back into Emily's eyes, I said, "It'll take you *maybe* five minutes to take the trip over there with your sisters. It won't kill you."

"You sure it won't?" Emily responded. "Because I could trip and fall and die or something. Plus, he could be a total weirdo and into kids, and you're sending all your girls over to his house."

"Stop," I said, furrowing my eyes. "It'll be fine. Newport is a good town with good people. I met him and he's fine." Leading my girls out the back door and onto the bricked patio, I sent them next door.

Returning to the kitchen, I poured myself a cup of tea from the kettle on the stove and went to the patio—my favorite place. I could look out across the lake and drink in a beautiful sunset in the evenings and also look up at the starry night sky on a cloudless night while I kept warm by my outdoor fireplace. No matter the night or occasion, I found comfort in being able to see and appreciate God's design and handiwork in all the beauty from the patio. *If only there were someone to share it with.*

Turning my eyes to the sky, I raised my cup of tea

toward Heaven and said, "Thank you for getting me through another day, Lord." As the tea rushed over my taste buds like a high tide coming in, I felt my body relax and my mind begin to unwind.

After a while—enough time to be concerned—I began to wonder why the girls hadn't come back yet. Standing up, I walked over and glanced through the evening toward the light I could see illuminated on Dylan's back porch. *Why aren't they back yet?* Anxiously waiting, I kept my eyes on the light. A few more minutes passed, and then I decided to walk over and see what was going on.

Walking up to the back porch, I took a deep breath and let it escape my lips. It helped lower the anxious feelings that were churning in my chest. Giving the door a couple of short knocks, I waited. I could hear little footsteps coming to the front door, and little

Bailey opened it.

"Mommy!" she said with a twinkle in her eye.

"You've gotta come see this!" she exclaimed, grasping onto my hand and leading me into the house.

"See what?" I asked with a smile as she led me through a hallway and to a stairwell.

"Upstairs. These birds!"

"Birds?"

"Yes! Birds! Dylan makes them out of wood. He has lots of them!"

"All right. Let's go see."

Bailey took me upstairs and down a hallway of doors to an open one. Inside, I found Emily and Tristan at the base of a chair that Dylan was sitting in. In his hands, he held a small bluebird sitting perched on a barbed-wire fence.

"You were right," Emily said, making eye contact with me for a moment and then over to Dylan. "It was her."

His eyes met mine as he grinned. "Sorry, Charlotte. I didn't mean to worry you. They were just fascinated with one of my carvings down in the kitchen."

I smiled and shook my head. "It's all right. So you carved all these?" My eyes scanned the shelves that were full of different types of birds. "They are all so life-like."

"I love birds. They're not only beautiful, but such a staple of the Christian faith." My heart fluttered and my smile grew wider at his words. *A man of God?* How'd I get so lucky with the new neighbor next door? Was it divine or just pure luck?

Emily stood up and said, "I'm going home." As she began to leave, Tristan and Bailey joined her.

Dylan stood and smiled as they exited.

"The bird verse is in Matthew, right?" I asked as he came over to me.

He nodded. "There are a lot of verses about birds in the Scriptures, but the one you're probably thinking of is Matthew 6:26. 'Look at the birds of the air; they do not sow or reap or store away in barns, and yet your heavenly Father feeds them. Are you not much more valuable than they?' "

Slowly nodding I replied, "Yes." He placed the bird he had in my hands. As I smoothed my thumb across the textures, I thought about the precise attention to detail that must have been required.

"How long have you been carving?"

"Three decades."

My eyes widened.

"My father taught me how to whittle when I was old enough not to cut myself with a knife."

As I handed the bird back to him, our hands touched. Even though it was for less than a second, what felt like a surge of electricity shot through my body. Judging by the look on his face, he felt it too. He smiled at me and then placed the bird back on the shelf.

As we walked down the narrow, creaky stairwell back downstairs, my foot suddenly went through one of the steps, and Dylan caught me in his arms as I let out a screech. Pulling me back up to the step he was on, he held me close to his chest for a moment before releasing.

"You okay?" he asked. We both gazed at the broken step.

"Yeah . . . is that a room?" I asked as we both looked into a dark, open space that was sending up the distinct aroma of old.

He shook his head slowly. "I don't know, but let's find out. That is . . . unless you have to get back home?"

I shook my head. "They'll be okay. Emily's sixteen."

Dylan smiled and took me by the hand to help me over the broken step. He led me through the living room and out into the garage. As we stepped into the garage, he said, "Those stairs run along the side of this wall." His fingers tapped the wall as he glanced over the barren wall.

"Maybe it was sealed off?"

Pressing his lips together tightly, he looked to be contemplating something. "I don't know." He glanced to the door. "There's one more place."

We went back into the house and to a room on the other side that was parallel to the garage. Standing in the doorway, we both looked around the empty room that only had a box in it. My eyes fell on a raised area of the wall. Walking over to it, I smoothed my fingers over it. "Dylan?" I questioned as I turned my head to him as he was further down on the wall.

He came over and touched the wall. As he let his fingers glide across the wall, he looked at me. Then he grinned. "There was a door right here." He jumped up and took a step back. "I'm going to go get my sledgehammer and knock it down."

As I waited for him to return, I looked at the box in the room. Curious, I walked over to it and saw the name, *Elise*, in a thick black marker written on the side. Who was Elise? I began to wonder. Glancing toward the doorway of the room, I listened to see if he was coming back—he wasn't. The box was already opened, and the flaps were already undone. *Just a peek won't hurt.* Lifting a flap with a single finger, I peeked in. Seeing a pink Ms. Wisconsin pageant sash, I let the flap fall and backed away. My nerves skyrocketed and I looked nervously to the doorway of the room again. *One more peek.* Going back to the box, I looked again. I saw a picture of Dylan and this *Elise*. My heart began to race.

"What are you doing?" Dylan asked as he stood in the doorway with his sledgehammer in hand.

Backing up away from the box, I apologized. "I'm so sorry. I just saw the name . . . and I was curious. I just—" Pressing my hand against my forehead, I shook my head. "I."

He set the sledgehammer against the wall and stepped closer to me. Touching the side of my arm, he shook his head. "I understand. I'd do the same thing."

"Really?"

He nodded. "Elise was my wife."

"You said you didn't have a wife."

"I don't." His eyes went to the box. "Not anymore."

I wanted to know what happened, but I didn't want to push it. It wasn't right. Not on the first day of meeting someone. "I'm sorry to hear that."

"It's all right." He looked at me. "You ready to find out what's in that room?"

"Yeah!"

He grabbed the sledgehammer and we went over to the wall. He swung and put a hole right through the wall. Dropping the hammer, he scrunched down on his knees and peeked inside. I came over and got down next to him, resting my hand on his back as I glanced in.

"Nothing," he replied as he swiped his hands through the cobwebs. We both stood up and looked at each other.

I smiled. "Well, it was fun to look and see. I'd better get back."

He nodded. "Let me walk you out."

As we walked through his house and to the back porch, I couldn't help but feel a longing to stay longer. But I knew staying wouldn't be right. My girls needed me to be home, not out all night with the next door neighbor I just met. Kids were impressionable, and I didn't want that pressed into their minds.

As we opened the door and I stepped out, I glanced over his shoulder. "I'm kind of bummed there wasn't anything in that room. I'm kind of an 'old stuff' junky."

"Like history?" he asked.

I nodded. "I love history."

"I'm the same way."

Anxiety crept in as I knew our time together was about to end. "Would you like to come over for dinner? Tomorrow?" I asked. My nerves shook me to the core as I awaited his reply.

He smiled. "I'd like that. What time?" *Phew!*

"Six?"

"I'll be looking forward to it."

"Awesome. See you then!" I could hardly believe it. The gorgeous next door neighbor said 'yes' to dinner.

As I left Dylan's house that night and made my way back over to my porch, my footsteps had a little bit more of a bounce to them. This new neighbor was turning out to be one of the most interesting men I had met in a very long time—the woodcarving, the piano, and that fun room we stumbled upon. I barely knew the guy, but that didn't stop me from daydreaming of what life could be like with a man like him.

CHAPTER 4

Closing the bedroom door to the girls' room after putting Bailey and Tristan down to sleep, I heard a knock come from downstairs. Emily was at a friend's house for the night. Answering the door, I was surprised to see it was my younger sister, Abby. Her mascara was running down her cheeks and her eyes were bloodshot.

"What's wrong?" I asked as I embraced her.

"Chase. He's gone for good this time." She released from our hug and went over to the couch, collapsing into the cushions.

Joining her on the couch, I placed a hand on Abby's shoulder. She was hurting, that was obvious, but I wasn't sure what had happened this time. I could've guessed it though. My sister did have the tendency of having a new flavor of boyfriend almost weekly. Well, it was more like every month, but still, she went through them faster than I could count. In the mere two years of living in Newport, she had over fifteen that I could recall off the top of my head. She was a sad and lonely soul, never able to settle on one man and always looking for love in all the worst places. For the longest time, I thought she just had a run of bad luck, but then last summer happened. She dated a guy named Peter. He was perfect for her—good job, kind, cute, and no issues—but she ended up dumping him. In her own words, she said they had 'creative differences.' Not sure what that really meant when it came to a relationship. She never really divulged to me the *why*. Regardless, they didn't last, and all the boyfriends since then didn't either. Searching for the right words in the moment, I accidently phrased my words inconsiderately. "What happened with this one?"

The tears stopped, she sat up and furrowed her eyebrows my way. "Don't you sit over there and judge me, Ms. Charlotte!"

"Seriously. You're *this* upset about Chase? You were *literally* just with Hal like what, a month ago? I last longer between cycles than you do in some of these relationships. It's tiresome, Abby."

She smiled. "Rude!"

Touching her hand, I said, "Come have some tea with me and tell me what happened. We need to go out back though. My girls are trying to sleep."

She nodded and wiped her eyes. Abby and I had a weird sister relationship. Sometimes, we were brutally honest. Other times, we were the sweetest little angels to each other. No matter what, we didn't let words or emotions get in the way of our sister-friendship. We got in a big fight once when I was still with Bradley, but we made a vow when I moved back to Newport never to let it happen again.

As we took our cups of tea out back onto the patio, I shut the door behind us. Abby sat down and placed her cup on the patio table that sat between our chairs.

"So what happened with Chase was . . . he wanted kids and a family and the whole *life* thing."

Taking a seat in the chair parallel to hers, I shook my head.

"What?"

Making eye contact with her, I said, "You broke up

with Hal because he didn't want that exact thing,
Abby. You see the problem here? You *want* that life .
. . why would you break up with this guy? Chase has
a son already and you were telling me how much
you loved being a mother role model to the kid.
Nothing lines up."

She dropped her face into her palms and began to
sob. "I guess I just don't know what I want!" She
sniffled.

"Well . . . why *don't* you want to have kids and a
family?"

She stopped crying and took a drink of her tea.
Glancing back at my house and then at me, she said,
"This life isn't me, Sis. You like *never* sleep. I need
my beauty sleep! You don't get looking this beautiful
without a lot of sleep in life."

"You're such a brat." I laughed. "My life is painful at times." A smile began to cross my face as I thought of my girls. "But it's so worth it, Abby. To be able to watch your children grow up and become young ladies . . . there's nothing like it on this earth. I know you're aware of how hard it's been since Bradley left me, but I wouldn't change my life for the world. There's something magical about looking into the eyes of your own child. Your own flesh and blood."

"Before or after they vomit, pee and poop all over you?" Abby laughed while I only flashed a courtesy smile. "Sorry. I know how much the girls mean to you, Charlotte." She set her cup down and brought her hands together in her lap as she peered up at the night sky. "I just don't know why God won't let me find peace over the right thing to do in life."

"God won't force you into finding peace, Abby. But

He *can* help you get through the trials and storms. Plus, I think there is peace that comes in choosing the right thing to do in God's eyes."

Abby looked at me and then over at the empty fireplace. "You should really build a fire more often."

Joining her gaze over at the sad, unlit fireplace, I nodded. "I know."

"Hey," Abby said abruptly. I looked over at her as she continued. "Thanks for being a good older sister."

I smiled. "Thanks for letting me flip you a little grief without you getting all upset about it."

She laughed. "You keep it real! I like that." Abby laughed. "I need that in my life. You're more like a best friend than a sister."

A pot with flowers suddenly fell over onto the porch. Glancing over, I saw Dylan in the light of the porch light. "Sorry. I didn't mean to interrupt!" Dylan said as he waved a hand and held a plate in his other.

Abby and I both jumped. His brown eyes caught my attention. "It's okay. You didn't interrupt." My eyes stayed fixed on his.

Abby cleared her throat, causing me to glance over at her and realize she wanted an introduction.

I stood up with Abby and introduced the two of them to each other. "Dylan, this is Abby, my sister. Abby, this is Dylan, the new neighbor next door."

As they shook hands, I could almost feel my chances with Dylan evaporate into the night sky that hung above Diamond Lake. Abby was always the prettier one of us girls growing up. And as anyone could guess, she was the one who would *always* land the guy. I clung to a thread of hope in the moment, though, as I saw Dylan quickly pull his hand away and turn his focus back to me. Handing me the plate that the cookies were on earlier, he smiled. "I didn't know if you might need this back tonight."

"If I needed a plate?" I let out a playful laugh. "I have a cupboard full."

He grinned and rubbed his neck as a smile crept into the corner of his mouth. "I guess that's probably true."

It was strange that he came over after I had just seen him not too long ago, but Dylan came across as genuine and innocent. I wasn't used to seeing that in a man.

"Want me to bring anything for dinner tomorrow?"

Dylan offered. I knew when the mention of dinner came off his lips that my sister had already begun her devilish plan to steal him away.

"I'll be there too, Dylan." Abby beamed with a smile, interrupting as she kept her eyes on Dylan. Looking over at Dylan, he didn't seem to care much. He was still looking at me. Each second that passed with our eyes on one another sent waves of happiness through me.

I pulled my eyes from his gaze for fear of awkwardness setting in. Finally, I replied to his question. "Don't worry about bringing anything over. I have it handled." While I did find comfort in the fact that Dylan was focused on me, I couldn't help but feel a bit agitated with my sister. Glancing over to her, I asked, "Is your boyfriend, Chase, going to be joining us, Abby?"

"No." She jerked her head in my direction. "We aren't together anymore, *Charlotte.*"

"Oh. That's right. You broke up today."

Dylan must have sensed the tension out on the patio as he took a step back and said, "I'm going to get going. I'll see you two tomorrow though?"

"See you then, Dylan," I replied.

"Looking forward to it!" added Abby as Dylan took his leave back to his house.

Abby was boy-crazy, but I had a good feeling about Dylan. He didn't seem swayed by her flirting and gorgeous looks. I came to the conclusion that, in a way, I was almost glad she was there that night. Abby was able to help me determine if he was worth my time or not. With three girls who had already been through enough, wasting another moment on a loser wouldn't be good for any of us.

CHAPTER 5

The next morning, I decided to enjoy my cup of coffee out on my patio in the hope of possibly seeing Dylan again. I had spent half the night dreaming about him while I tossed and turned. There was no getting those golden-brown eyes out of my head. Sitting down in my chair as I heard a few birds chirp overhead, I watched them for a moment as they landed on my yard over in the tree line that separated Mrs. Craig's and my property. Glancing down at the ground below the trees, I saw the eyesore that had been haunting me for weeks—yard debris from the big storm that had recently hit Newport. It had been a while since the storm, and I still hadn't made the time to clean up the debris. I always had an excuse not to do it, but now I had an excuse to do it. If I hung outside long enough, I might be able to catch a glimpse of Dylan.

After my cup of coffee, I went inside and put on a pair of overalls and grabbed my gardening gloves. When I came back out, I noticed Dylan sitting in a lawn chair near the edge of his dock, just beyond where his boat was docked. Taking a few steps toward him, I turned and decided against talking to him. I didn't want to come off like a stalker since I knew he hadn't been out there for more than a few minutes. As I walked off the opposite side of the patio and headed past the tire swing in my yard, I glanced back at him again and saw what looked to be a Bible in his hands. It warmed my heart when I saw it. A man was hard to find at my age, but a man who sought God was likened to that long lost bell in the bottom of Diamond Lake—nearly impossible to find. Smiling as I continued onward to the mess in my yard, I couldn't stop stealing glances back toward him. He was so perfect, I felt like God might have finally heard my prayers.

Gathering armfuls of branches, I hauled them across the yard to my burn pile near the shore where the grass turned to sand. As I hauled more debris, I began to wonder what Dylan's story was. Why did he move here? What happened to his wife? For a moment, I decided I was going to go talk to him, but a few paces into the journey, I once again changed my mind. I didn't want to interrupt his time with God, and he'd be over for dinner later in the evening anyway. On one of my final trips to the burn pile, I noticed the lawn chair and Dylan were gone. I let a sorrowful sigh escape my lips as he must have retreated into his house.

"Good morning, Charlotte." Dylan's voice startled me from behind.

Pressing my hand against my chest as I turned to him, I said, "You scared me!"

"Sorry about that . . ." His eyes went over to my burn pile. "Need a hand?"

Shaking my head, I glanced toward the tree line in my yard. "Mostly done now, but thanks for the offer."

He nodded and was turning around to leave when my thoughts went back to the assumption he was reading his Bible. "What were you reading?"

A smile peeked in from the corner of his lip as he turned to me. "My Bible."

"I thought that's what it was . . . which book?"

"A few different ones. I'm on the 'read the Bible in a year' track. I've been doing it every year for five years."

"Oh, wow. That's neat. I've done that once before, but it was a long time ago when I was with Bradley." Panic set in as I realized I mentioned my ex-husband. *Way to go, Charlotte!* Seeing Dylan's eyebrow go up, I knew he wanted to know who it was. "He's my ex-husband. He left me and the girls a couple of years ago." My face went red with embarrassment. "I'm sorry. I'm talking too much."

He raised a hand. "I understand, Charlotte. I was married too. You know that. No need to apologize."

"Thanks. It was pretty overwhelming, doing the yearly reading when I fell behind a couple of days. I remember that much."

He laughed. "Yeah. I've been there! I missed three days once because I was super busy with a work project and it was painful to catch back up. Overall, though, it's great. I feel like God reveals new truths every time I read, even though I've been through it so many times now."

I nodded as my heart warmed with joy. To hear a man speak in a positive light about God and the Scriptures was a breath of fresh air. Even though Bradley read the Bible in a year with me, he didn't care much about anything to do with God. Sure, he went to church, but he never had passion when it came to God. He always went through the motions, but he lacked the love. "I love how God can reveal new things to us each time we read His Word."

"It's truly divine how He works," Dylan replied.

Our conversation was cut short when my back door flung open and Tristan began to holler out to me. "Mom! Emily locked herself in the bathroom and said she's not opening the door. I'm supposed to go on a bike ride with Chrissy in a half hour!"

Peering over my shoulder, I said, "Be there in a second, dear." Connecting my eyes back with Dylan, we both shared a smile. "I'm beginning to think my girls just wait to interrupt our conversations."

He laughed. "Seems that way." His eyes turned to my house. "Guess you'd better get back to saving the world?"

"One meltdown at a time," I responded with a grin. We parted ways.

As I stepped onto the patio, I turned and looked back at Dylan. He was looking at me too. The feelings I was already beginning to feel for this guy were a bit unnerving. I needed to slow it down a tad, take a step back, and keep a good perspective. I didn't know him very well, and he wasn't married anymore—probably for a reason. I had more than myself to worry about. The last thing I needed in my life was another heartache and a broken dream. While taking it slower with my emotions was the right thing to do, my heart didn't want to agree.

CHAPTER 6

While the water on the stove boiled, I could feel my anxiety doing the same inside of me. It wouldn't be long before Dylan and Abby would be joining us for dinner. Staring at the clock on the stove as I waited for my water to boil, a welcomed distraction came in the form of a phone call from Edith.

Picking up the phone, I turned around and stared through the doorway that led into the living room. "Hello?"

"*Charlotte.* Tell me. What new information have you found out about the Atkins?"

The water came to a boil just then, and I grabbed for the noodles on the counter. Emptying the bag into the pot, I replied, "Nothing. I'm off work today. Been spending time just relaxing at home with the girls."

"I see. I heard today that the Atkins are gutting the inside of *The Newport Theater* entirely! Word on the street says they're repainting the walls and completely modernizing it inside. I'm so distraught!"

"They're going to paint over the Townson mural?" My eyebrows furrowed. "Jeez! That's even low for them! It's been a part of Newport forever!" My anger warmed as my noodles boiled on the stove.

In a troubled and worried voice, Edith replied, "I know. I don't like it. I don't like it one bit, Charlotte." She let out a sigh. "And I'm afraid they'll have my family's bell in no time! I'm so upset."

Sensing her hopelessness, I recalled what the Scriptures say about treasure. "Don't let yourself forget that the treasures we store up in heaven no thieving Atkin can ever touch. I don't know how much that helps . . ."

"It does help, Charlotte. That's why I like talking to you. You *always* have a way of helping my troubled soul find some comfort."

A single knock came from the front door and then it opened—it was Abby. Seeing her walk in, I wrapped up the call with Edith and called for Abby to come into the kitchen.

As she walked in, she set a bottle of wine on the counter. Seeing the bottle irritated me a little as she knew I didn't drink. Sensing my disdain for it, she glared at me and said, "Calm down, Sis. It's not for you. It's for me and Dylan."

"Whatever." Returning to preparing dinner, I pulled the chicken from the crockpot and placed it on the counter. As I began to shred it for the chicken noodle soup, I heard one of the girls come down the stairs.

"When's dinner?" Bailey asked, coming into the kitchen.

Glancing at her for a moment, I said, "Soon. I'm making it right now."

Another knock came from the door.

Abby leapt up from her seat to go answer it. "That's Dylan. I'll get it."

Rolling my eyes as I finished shredding the chicken, I set it aside and pulled the noodles from the stove. Steam came up from the pot as I combined the chicken, noodles and broth together. Abby and Dylan walked into the kitchen together, and I noticed he had a silver tray with tin foil wrapped over the top.

"I brought dessert." He lifted it up slightly. "Can I put it in the fridge?"

"I said you didn't need to bring anything, ya goof! But yeah, go ahead," I replied with a grin. Motioning with my head to the fridge, I continued, "You cook?" I asked with a raised eyebrow.

He nodded as he got into the fridge. "Hardly. It's banana cream pie. Pudding and graham crackers."

Abby interjected. "That's cooking. And it's awesome that you cook, Dylan."

If Abby kept it up this way and he actually *believed* what she said, he'd have a head the size of Texas before the night was over. Turning to Bailey, I said, "Go get your sisters. It's time for dinner."

Heading into the living room to grab the leaf insert for the table, I heard Abby asking Dylan what he did for work. As I moved the couch to pull the insert out, the girls came down the stairs.

"I'm pretty excited about it," Dylan said in response to Abby as I walked back into the kitchen with the insert and the girls. He helped me set the insert and then made eye contact with me. "We need extra chairs?"

"Patio chairs are fine. I'll grab them."

"No. I'll get 'em," he replied.

"Thank you."

Dylan slipped out the back door to get chairs, shutting it behind him.

Abby bumped my shoulder as I brought bowls of

soup over to the table as the girls sat down. "Can you believe he bought *The Newport Theater*?"

My face went flush and my heart began to pound. *He's an* Atkin? Setting the bowls in my hands down, I returned to the counter and clutched it. Disbelief swarmed my thoughts. How I felt about Dylan and what I knew about him were contrary to what I knew about the Atkins. Trying to find the words to put together to tell Abby he was an Atkin was interrupted when the back door opened and Dylan came in with chairs. Watching him as he put the chairs in place around the table, my feelings fought each other. I liked him *a lot,* but his being an Atkin scared me beyond belief.

"Do you want to take us on your cool boat?" Bailey asked Dylan as he sat down. I began to feel queasy as I realized my children were already becoming fond of him.

"Honey. That's too forward," I said gently to her. Coming over to the table, I set her bowl down in front of her and one in front of Tristan.

"No. No. It's fine." Dylan unfolded his napkin and set it in his lap. "I'd love to take you all boating sometime. It'd be fun."

I let out a nervous laugh as my feelings for Dylan collided with my hatred for the Atkins.

"What's so funny about that? Did I miss something?" Abby asked as she sat down next to Dylan at the table and looked at me inquisitively.

"Nothing. Sorry." My mind was racing a million miles a second. I needed to get this guy out of my life and I needed to tell Edith it was my neighbor that was the new Atkin cousin in town. My relationship with Edith and the Townsons stretched back into my youth, but Dylan and I stretched back a singular day. But how could I? How could I peel away in the middle of dinner for a phone call? Or what about kicking him out? I couldn't cause a scene like that in front of the girls. They'd think I was a lunatic, especially since they had no idea about my viewpoints on the Atkins family or what they did to the Townsons so many years ago. Sure, they had heard of the feud in school, but when they questioned me about it, I remained neutral and dismissive of the topic. While I did feel strongly about the Atkins, I never divulged my ill-willed feelings to my children. I felt that wouldn't be right of me.

Abby got up a few minutes into the meal and retrieved the wine from the counter, along with two wine glasses from the cupboard that had been given to Bradley and me as wedding gifts years ago. Coming back to her seat, she sat down and poured herself and Dylan a glass of wine. Knowing she shared the same feelings about the Atkins made it hard not to laugh in the moment as I watched her try to pursue him. In my mind, she could have him now. I couldn't betray the Townsons like that. Dylan shook his head and pushed the wine glass away.

"I don't drink," he replied.

Making eye contact with Bailey across the table, I said, "Honey. Would you please bless the food?"

"Yes, Mommy." Bowing her head and folding her hands together, she prayed. "Dear God. Thank you for the food. Thank you for the day. Thank you for the cook. Thank you for Dylan being here. Thank you for Aunt Abby being here. Amen!"

As dinner continued, I watched with worry as all my girls seemed to be fascinated with the stories Dylan told them. He told stories of far-off lands where princesses and knights lived and even a story about the spookiest hotel in a ghost town that he had visited in the middle of nowhere over in the Montana mountains. They liked him so much, and it pained me to watch it unfold.

Trying to push off the fact that he was an Atkin, I kept up my act the best that I could until I slipped on a question that Bailey asked him.

"Where'd you get that awesome gold nugget you showed us that was on the fireplace?"

"I found it," he responded.

"Sure you didn't steal it?" I asked snidely. The table

fell so quiet in the moment following that, a mouse could have scurried across the floor and we would have heard the little footsteps it made. Awkward silence filled the room until it was about to burst.

"Don't be so rude to Dylan," Abby responded, shaking her head as she looked over at Dylan with eyes of desire and touched his arm.

"Oh for crying out loud, Abby!" I retorted with a laugh. "He's an Atkin!"

Abby's eyebrows furrowed over at Dylan and she retracted her hand. Jumping up from my seat, I headed out to the back patio and slammed the door behind me in frustration with myself. Abby followed me outside.

"How'd you find that out?" she pressed. "And why on earth did you not tell me?"

"An Atkin purchased *The Newport Theater*. Edith told me that a while ago, and you said he bought it. I just put two and two together."

Pressing her hand against her forehead, she shook her head with a longing look back toward the door. "I was *really* beginning to like this one."

"You like every guy!" I snapped back. "Sorry. I'm just furious right now. I don't date. You know that, and I truly liked him." Walking past Abby to go back inside, she pressed my shoulder to stop me.

"I'm sorry."

My eyes welled with tears as my throat felt as if it were closing. "It's fine." Placing my hand on the doorknob to open it, Abby grabbed my shoulder again.

"What are you doing, Sis?"

"I'm going to kick him out of my house. I was trying to avoid a scene, but a scene has been made now. Might as well finish it off before my daughters fall for him anymore." Sidestepping from her hand, I continued inside. Looking straight at Dylan, our eyes met and I was about to yell, but stopped. Instead, I just stared at him.

Dylan dipped his chin, wiped his mouth with his napkin and stood up. Dropping the napkin into his bowl, he looked at me. "Thank you for dinner." Stepping away from the table, he headed toward the door and walked away without a word. As I shut the door behind him, I felt a bit of regret close with it.

"Um . . . what was *that*?" Emily asked.

"Don't worry about it," I replied as I came over and retrieved his bowl to put in the sink.

She stood up. "*What?* You just kicked him out. I don't understand what he did!"

"I said don't worry about it, Emily! I am your mother and I know what is best!" My voice was firm, which wasn't normal, so she backed off. Taking her bowl to the sink, she dropped it in and went upstairs to her room. Bailey and Tristan followed suit.

Abby took her bottle of wine and left, and I was alone at the kitchen table. Left to figure out what had just happened. Why did Dylan hide that fact? Was he trying to trick me into liking him? I could see the Atkins doing something like that, but Dylan? The woodcarving, God-fearing man? My eyes drifted over to the window that looked out into the darkness between our houses. Do I call and rat him out to Edith? Shaking my head, I pressed my hand against my forehead and mulled over the fact that he was an Atkin. *What am I supposed to do now,*

God?

CHAPTER 7

Over the next three days of work, I tossed around the idea of calling Edith but never went through with it. Without a peep from Dylan next door and no real reason to tell her, I figured it wasn't a big deal. One evening after work, while I was pulling into my driveway, I noticed a light flickered from the back of my house. *Did my mother build a fire with the girls?* Parking, I got out and ventured toward the back of my house. Rounding the corner, I smiled as I saw the fire roaring in the fireplace and my mother sitting with a cup of tea in her hands.

"Wow. I gotta say I'm impressed, Mother." I set my purse down on the seat of one of the patio chairs and approached my mother as she glanced back at me.

"How was work?" she asked.

"Good . . . Serenah came in for a pick up. I guess the inn is hopping pretty good this summer. She's going to have their wedding in August. Right at the inn."

"Oh, that should be neat."

I was about to ask if Emily had come back from her friend's house when the back door opened and she came outside. To my surprise, Dylan was right behind her. Taking a step back, I furrowed my eyebrows as I made eye contact with him. "What are you doing here?"

Emily took a step toward me. "It's fine, Mom. He helped build us a fire and—"

I cut her off as I asked Dylan, "Could we talk?"

Pursing his lips as he nodded, he joined me to step away from the patio and out of earshot of my mom and daughter.

As we came out into the yard, I laid into him. "What are you trying to do, Dylan? This is *my* family!"

"I just thought—"

"Thought what? I kicked you out of my house! You *thought* it'd be fine to come around my house and my girls, and when I'm not around? Like you just need to avoid me?" My anger waxed hotter with every word. His true Atkins heritage was beginning to shine. "I don't want you around here!"

He stayed quiet and shook his head, trying to contain a smile.

I smacked him. "What?"

"This is *all* because I'm an Atkin?"

"Yeah!" I snapped. "Edith Townson has been a very close family friend, and what your family—"

He put a hand up. "Stop. I get it, *Charlotte*. What some distant relatives of mine *supposedly* did a long time ago somehow has something to do with me." Shaking his head, he continued as he made eye contact with me. "You know, I thought you were different. But I guess you're just like the rest of them—*petty*. I am sure God is pretty proud of you right now." I could feel the disappointment as he looked into my eyes and then turned away to steal a glance at the patio before heading back to his house.

Hating that he was right, I glared into the shifting darkness as he crossed over onto his property. Letting out a sigh, I looked up and prayed for God to change my heart. God needed to take this over, but my emotional response system didn't care about what I knew was right. There was a gnawing feeling inside of me that told me the Atkins were trouble. I turned and headed back around the patio.

"How could you treat him like that, Mom?" Emily pressed as I came back up to where she and my mother were sitting.

"You're but a child, Emily. I don't have to explain things to you."

She stood up and stormed inside, slamming the door behind her.

My mother glanced over at me as I shook my head. "Why must you treat him so poorly, Charlotte?"

"He's an Atkin, Mom."

She slowly nodded and then turned her eyes to the crackling fire. "Emily's friend stayed for a while earlier when she came over to drop her off. They were both swinging on the tire swing and it broke mid-swing. Dylan was outside working on his deck when it happened, and he rushed over . . . he fixed it for them."

"You asked him to do that?"

My mother shook her head. "Of course not. He just did it, and then we got to talking. I invited him to stay for supper since he fixed the tire swing. Atkin or not, he's a *very* nice man."

Shrugging, I let out a sigh. "Doesn't really matter anymore." My eyes wandered next door to his back porch light. "He probably hates me."

"Well, you kicked him off your property when you

got home . . ."

"I didn't know the story."

"That's right. You didn't. Atkin, Townson dramas aside . . . do you like him?"

I looked over at her as I felt tears well in my eyes. I nodded. "I do."

"Don't lose sight of that truth."

A weird feeling settled over me. I felt wrong about not liking him based on his family name, but some part of me fought against that logic. The Atkins family had a long running history of wrongdoings and they were never good people. Dylan's statement of me being like the rest of them pressed against my mind. Was he right? Was I wrong? Maybe it was my firsthand experience of dating an Atkin that kept a hold on me. I had dated one in high school. First, they sweet talk you. Then they make you feel special. Then they drop you off on highway 101 blindfolded and you have to walk ten miles back to town on the same night of your Commencement dance. Could Dylan really be different? And more importantly, was that a risk I was willing to take?

After my mother left and I got the girls tucked into their beds, I headed out to my patio for my rendezvous with the stars and my cup of hot tea. While I wasn't happy that Dylan was over at my house when I got home earlier, I couldn't resist the feeling of thankfulness for the warmth of the fireplace that evening.

As I cozied up in my chair in front of the fireplace outside, I brought my knees to my chest and took a sip of my tea. My eyes scanned across the horizon of the moonlit lake and took a moment to appreciate God's handiwork. The only sound that I could hear was the sound of the water lapping against the shore and my heartbeat.

A half hour passed as I prayed and meditated on Scriptures. Then a break in the quiet came. That baby grand piano I saw being moved into Dylan's house suddenly started playing next door. The sweet sounds strummed the strings of my aching heart and brought calmness over me. Relaxing my head against the back of my chair, I glanced over to Dylan's house as I continued listening. Then First Corinthians 13:1 came to my thoughts. *If I speak in tongues of men or angels, but do not have love, I am only a resounding gong or a clanging cymbal.* Then I felt the Spirit focus in on part of the verse, replaying it in my mind . . . *but do not have love.* Whether I wanted to be with Dylan or not, I needed to show love. It didn't matter how well I prayed at church in the women's prayer group. It didn't matter how well I did anything for God. If I didn't have love, God's love, I had nothing.

The piano stopped playing and a void was left in the evening air that wasn't there before. The sounds of crashing waves on the shore no longer brought peace to my soul. Emptiness surrounded me. I needed to make amends with Dylan and I needed to show God's love, but I didn't know if I could.

CHAPTER 8

The next morning, I saw Dylan through the window in my kitchen. He was sitting in his chair out on the dock. I knew what I had to do. Wrapping my robe tightly around my waist, I headed out the back door and over to him.

My mind raced with how to word the apology on my way over to him, but I drew a sudden blank as I stood behind him and he turned to look at me. His brown eyes no longer held the joy I once saw in them. He looked to be plagued with a grief I had no understanding of.

"Dylan . . ." I managed to get out.

"What, Charlotte?" he asked. When I didn't say anything, he turned back to his Bible and the lake as he remained in his seat.

"I'm sorry." When he didn't look back at me or respond, I decided to turn and leave him on the dock. I was frustrated, not with him, but with myself for letting myself hold his family name against him.

Leaving the dock, I headed back to my house as tears welled in my eyes. I did everything I could. Now it was up to God.

After work, I picked up the kids from the house and took them over to Abby's for the barbecue she was having. My mother was coming too. As I pulled into the driveway of her house, I saw a few extra cars parked outside. *Wonder who she invited?* My impression was that the barbecue was a family get-together, but that didn't look to be the case.

As the girls and I got out of the car, Emily asked, "How long do we have to be here? I wanted to go hang out with Brianna tonight."

"Hush," I replied as we all headed toward the gate on the side of the house.

Coming into the backyard, I saw Chase barbecuing burgers and hot dogs while Abby brought paper plates and napkins out to the picnic table. She glanced over at me and flashed a big smile before coming over.

"I'm so happy you're here, Sis!" she said, approaching and then wrapping her arms around me for a big hug. "Have you heard from Mom?"

"She should be here soon . . ." I replied as I glanced over her shoulder at Chase. "What's he doing here?"

Abby grinned. "We're back together."

I nodded with raised eyebrows.

She shook her head. "We're getting married and moving to Seattle. Chase got a job with some big software company."

Married? Was she nuts? "Oh."

"I'm going to be okay. Things are good now." She glanced over at someone I didn't know who was helping Chase's little boy on the monkey bars. "I spent some time with Pastor Charles. He taught me a lot about how much God values me and I just get it now. I'm not so worried about the future anymore. Once I stopped thinking about myself, everything just made sense."

"Honestly . . . I didn't know you were saved."

She shoved my shoulder playfully. "I made that commitment to Christ at church camp when I was a teenager. Don't you remember?"

Shaking my head, I said, "No."

"Yeah. I got baptized and everything at camp. Anyway . . . I don't know if I was *really* saved or not then, since Jesus wasn't ever the Lord of my life, but I made a recommitment to Christ a couple of days ago."

I smiled. "Good to hear, Abby." While I wasn't sure about her decisions with moving, marriage and even Chase, I was sure of the decision for Christ. I was proud of her for making the commitment.

Mother walked into the backyard, interrupting our conversation and we both looked at her.

Leaning into Abby's ear, I asked, "Did you tell our mother yet?"

"Nope."

Smiling, I looked at Abby. "Have fun with that." Leaving them, I went over to the barbecue and talked to Chase while Abby told mom about the big change in her life.

CHAPTER 9

Weeks came and went without a word from Dylan. He was the neighbor I no longer spoke to and only saw when he would come and go from his house. He continued to play the piano in the evenings, and I'd make sure I was out on my patio to listen. My conscience and the Spirit tortured me daily over what had transpired between us. I called myself a Christian, but I hadn't acted like one with him. One day, after a mid-shift at work, I decided to go talk to him again, this time at *The Newport Theater*'s construction site. After a longwinded prayer earlier that morning, which resulted in an emotional breakdown, I felt as if God had whispered into my ear, *try again*. Parking alongside the curb at the construction site, I got out and scanned the workers who were coming in and out of the propped open doors just below the giant neon sign that read diagonally, *The Newport Theater*. My nerves were shooting off bits of electricity, and I felt my throat clasping shut. I was going from apologetic neighbor to full-fledged stalker with this action, but I had to try again.

My eyes bounced from face to face, and then I saw him. I could feel my heart skip a beat when my eyes fell on him for the first time in weeks. He was wearing a pair of jeans and a plain white tee shirt with a hard hat to top it all off. He looked tired and dirty from toiling the day away in the heat, but he looked good as usual.

God, help me. "Dylan!" I called out from across the street.

He turned and looked over at me after tossing a box he had in a dumpster. It was only for a moment, but I could feel his disappointment hiding behind his big brown eyes. It ripped me apart that he was still hurt by my actions. He headed back toward the entrance.

Glancing both directions, I darted across the street and over to the doors. Seeing him pick up a plank of wood inside and walk back toward my direction, I stood to the side of the door and waited for him. As he walked by, I joined his side. "Hey. I want to talk to you."

He stopped and looked over at me. "Ever think maybe I don't want to talk to you?" He continued on to the dumpster.

Joining his side again, I said, "I just want to see how

things are going. With *The Newport Theater* and . . . you know . . . everything . . ."

He laughed as he tossed the wood into the back of a nearby pickup truck. Turning around to face me, he looked at me with his piercing eyes. They tore through me and touched my soul, similar to the way his piano playing had been. "You came here to ask me how *The Newport Theater* is going?" He folded his arms. "You just want to sweep what you did under the rug?"

"I said I'm sorry, Dylan." I shook my head. "I don't know what more you want from me."

Another construction worker came up to him. "Dylan. We need you inside."

"Just a sec," Dylan responded to the man. He looked back at me. "You know, Charlotte. You should read up on Ephesians 4:31. It'd be a great insight for you."

His tone had an air of superiority to it that just

rubbed me the wrong way. He gently touched my

shoulder, sending sparks shooting all over my body,

and then went on his way.

Crossing the street to my car, I racked my mind

trying to think of the verse and the fact that he just

told me to go read my Bible. Who did he think he

was? Just telling me to go read my Bible. I knew I'd

be upset no matter what the Scripture said. Once I

got in my car, I pulled my phone out and looked up

the verse.

Get rid of all bitterness, rage and anger, brawling and

slander, along with every form of malice. Ephesians

4:31

I had already admitted that I was in the wrong. I didn't feel the verse was very applicable to the situation. Glancing out my window toward *The Newport Theater*, I thought about how self-righteous that move was on his part. *Maybe I don't like this guy as much as I thought I did.* Looking back down at my phone, I was about to exit the app when I saw the next verse.

Be kind and compassionate to one another, forgiving each other, just as in Christ God forgave you.

Ephesians 4:32

I laughed. *That's perfect!* I loved the fact that the verse followed right after the one he brought up to me. It was a God thing, that's for sure. If Dylan wanted to play the 'read this verse' game with me, I was going to give him a dose of his own medicine. As I grabbed the door handle, my phone rang—it was my mother. I paused from exiting the vehicle.

"Where are you? I need to be over to the museum in twenty minutes to meet Sandy."

I peered over at *The Newport Theater*. I needed to get home, but that didn't mean I wouldn't nail the verse to his door. "Sorry, Mom. I'm on my way home right now."

As I was clearing the table after dinner, a knock

came from the back door off the kitchen. Setting the handful of plates down in the sink, I went over to see who it was. Pulling the curtain back on the door's window, I saw it was Dylan.

Relief came over me as I opened the door. "*Dylan.*"

"You left something of yours on my door," he replied, stepping into the kitchen and holding up my note an inch in front of my eyes. I took a step back.

"I figured we were playing the whole *read this verse game.*" I let out a soft chuckle.

"*Okay*, Charlotte." He looked at the paper. "Verse thirty-two? You want to tell me about *forgiveness*? You held it against me that I was an Atkin. What about forgiveness for something that happened eons ago and that I didn't even do?"

"I tried to make amends. What do you do? You tell me to go read my Bible like you're some sort of God's gift to mankind."

He laughed. "You're cute!"

"What?" I replied, perplexed.

"Your nose. It curls up when you're mad." He smiled. "I know I probably seem hot and cold right now, but there's a lot of emotions going on inside of me right now." He stepped closer to me and took my hands in his. "Every night, I struggle knowing you're just a few steps away from me. It's torture, and I don't want to do it anymore, Charlotte. I like you. A lot."

"I like you too, Dylan . . ."

"What is it?"

Shaking my head, I replied, "I've listened to you play

the piano every evening, and you don't come across as struggling."

"You could hear me playing?"

I nodded.

"I haven't been able to play the piano since Elise passed away, but I finally was able to after I met you. Then after our fight, I played to help soothe my pained soul. You've made me feel things, Charlotte, that I thought I'd never feel again."

My eyes welled with tears at his words. He wasn't divorced. His wife had died. Tingles of sadness pierced through my body and my throat tightened as he exposed his heart for the first time to me.

"Mommy . . ." Bailey said suddenly from the doorway of the kitchen, breaking through our conversation. Tristan was by her side.

I pulled my hands back from Dylan and turned to the girls as I dabbed the tears from my eyes. "What is it?"

Tristan nudged Bailey's shoulder, and she pulled her hand out from behind her back, revealing a piece of oddly sharpened drift wood. At second glance I spotted the town's seal on it. A small worked piece of metal that had been screwed into the wood. Though it was worn down, it was visible to the naked eye. *This has to be from the raft that carried the bell across the lake.* My eyes widened as I stepped closer. Taking it out of Bailey's hand, I began to inspect the piece of wood closely.

Dylan stepped beside me as he tried to peek, and I jerked my body in reflex. Everything inside me wanted to hide it, even though I knew he wasn't like the other Atkins. Glancing over my shoulder at

Dylan, my eyes met his and I recalled the Scripture that had pressed against my heart time and time again, starting with the first night he played the piano. *First Corinthians 13:1 - If I speak in tongues of men or of angels, but do not have love, I am only a resounding gong or a clanging cymbal.* I wasn't in love with Dylan, but *this* moment was my chance to show him God's love that existed inside me. Turning around to Dylan, I gave him the piece of paddle.

He rubbed a thumb over the engraved crest. His eyes grew wide. "Wow. I've only heard the stories handed down by the generations." He looked up at me. "I love the history of this town. It's so fascinating."

"I think so too."

He came over and stood partially behind me as he

brought his arm around my body and took my hand with the wood in it and brought it up in front of my eyes. "Look," he said, pressing his finger against the wood as his arm was wrapped around me. Though his touch was light, it fueled the desire I had for him, and his muscular arm around me felt safe— something I hadn't felt in years.

"What?" I asked as I squinted at the piece of wood.

"The intricate detail of the crest is incredible."

Smiling as I knew he was just making an excuse to get close to me again, I nodded. "Really neat."

"We found it on the shore. We'll show you!" Tristan said as she scurried toward the back door with Bailey.

Dylan handed me back the piece of wood and I pushed it back into his hands. "Keep it. It's part of your family's history."

As we stepped out onto the back patio, the warm summer evening air wrapped itself around us. I don't know if it was because Dylan and I had the talk or the fact that I finally felt a firm understanding of the guy, but I felt a sense of calm and peace wash over me.

Arriving down at the sand with the girls, they led us a little further down my side of the shore. As we followed behind them, Dylan reached over and grabbed my hand, causing a surge of warmth to go through my body. I couldn't stop smiling as we walked hand in hand on the shore that evening.

Stopping, the girls turned around and we released our hands. I loved that he understood me and didn't want to force the kids into the idea of an 'us' right then and there.

"This the spot?" I asked.

Bailey and Tristan nodded.

The girls ran back to the house, leaving Dylan and me alone on the shore. Raising my eyes to the still waters of the lake, I thought about Edith and her family. They could finally recover the bell after so long of not knowing where it had gone. "The Townsons will be able to recover the bell now."

Dylan looked over at me and asked, "Is that what you want?"

I turned to him to respond. "It is."

Dylan's eyes went back out to the lake, and the sound of nearby owl interrupted the quietness in the air. "Why ruin our beautiful backyards with boats and media for some earthly treasure?"

I looked over at him again as his eyes stayed fixed on the water. "You're right." Stepping closer to him, I laid my head against his shoulder and he wrapped his arm around my waist. Dylan didn't want anything to do with the feud, and neither did I.

CHAPTER 10

After an excruciating day at work the next day, I welcomed my cup of hot tea on the back patio. As I stepped out into evening, I saw the moon casting a beautiful reflection across the lake.

"Beautiful, isn't it?" Dylan asked suddenly as he came up onto the patio. He had surprised me, but what a handsome surprise. A soft blue flannel shirt and a pair of jeans that fit just right. He smiled warmly and I flashed him a smile. "Sorry. I didn't mean to startle you. Just saw you pull in a little bit ago and figured you might want to hang out."

I smiled. "You read my mind. Would you like some tea?"

"No thanks."

"Coffee?"

"Yeah. I'll take some if you have it."

"I'll brew some for you." I turned and headed back inside.

"I'll get a fire going," he said as he glanced over the darkened fireplace.

"Sounds good." I headed inside and couldn't help but smile as I prepared a half-pot of coffee.

Emily walked into the kitchen and stopped at the fridge to look over at me. "Could I have a soda?"

"Sure."

"Wait. Why are you so . . . smiley, Mom?" She tilted her head as suspicion crept across her face. "What's going on with you?"

The sound of Dylan dropping a piece of wood outside pulled Emily's attention. She hurried over to the door and looked through the curtain. A smile grew on her face. "Dylan's over. *Now* it makes sense."

I laughed. "We're just friends."

Emily nodded slowly as she went over to the fridge. "Okay, Mom."

"What?"

"Tristan told me she caught you two holding hands last night."

"Pshh . . ." I replied as I turned red.

"He's a good guy. We all like him."

"I'm not dating him, *Emily.*"

"Just sayin'." She took a soda from the fridge and headed out of the kitchen.

The half-pot of coffee was soon done, and I went back out to Dylan. As I came outside, Dylan struck a match and started the fire. He stood and joined me as I took a seat. As I handed him his cup of coffee, I said, "Thanks for starting the fire."

He smiled. "Thanks for the coffee." Taking a sip, he let out a long sigh and then set the cup down on the patio table. "You ever wonder if you had done something differently, what your life would have turned out to be like?"

After taking a sip of my tea, I set it down on the patio table between us and nodded. "All the time. What did *you* do wrong?"

He leaned forward in the chair as the reflection of

the fire danced across his face. Bringing his hands together between his knees, he rubbed them together and shook his head and kept his eyes fixed on the growing flames. "I already told you I lost my wife, but I didn't tell you my daughter was in the car."

His words were weighted with such grief and turmoil that I couldn't keep myself from feeling a part of his pain. As if a knife sliced through my chest and buried itself in my heart, I felt for him. "Wow. I'm so sorry, Dylan. I lost my father eight years ago and it was hard. Loss is difficult."

He rubbed his chin and lowered his head as his palm cupped the back of his neck, but he didn't speak a word.

"I'm sorry." My voice quieted. "I wasn't trying to say

I understood that pain. I couldn't imagine losing a child or a spouse."

He sat back in his chair and shook his head. Glancing over at me, he said, "It's okay. My head's been in the clouds all day. The reason I say any of this is because it's the anniversary of the wreck today." His eyes went back over to the fire as it let out a pop in the wood. "Three years ago."

Joining his gaze at the fire, I said, "When Bradley left me and the girls, I thought I was going to die. How much worse it's got to be for you . . . I can't even fathom it."

He raised a hand as he looked over at me. "That's where you're wrong, Charlotte. My wife and daughter didn't choose to leave. Yeah, what happened sucked, but that's nothing compared to a spouse wanting to leave." He shook his head and looked back at the flames dancing in the fireplace.

"True, but parents should never outlive their children."

He nodded. "That *part*—" He choked up on his words and shook his head as he bit his trembling lip.

A silence filled the air for a few moments. It was neither awkward nor comfortable. It was just silent. Then, suddenly, Dylan's hand found its way across the patio table and over to mine that sat on the armrest of the chair I was in. He smoothed his thumb over the top of my hand and looked at me. "You're doing a great job with those girls."

I hadn't heard that statement in a long time, if ever. It felt nice. "Thank you."

"Sometimes, I wonder how Jenny would be now.

She'd be close to Bailey's age, and it's hard to imagine her that old, honestly. She was always just my little girl."

"They stay little forever in your eyes. Even now, when I look at Emily . . . I see that sweet little four-year-old who couldn't stop trying on different princess dress up clothing every day." I turned my hand to hold his. Squeezing, I said, "You're a great guy, Dylan. I'm sure you were a great dad too."

"Thank you."

"Can I ask you something, Dylan? Honestly."

"Go for it."

I let out a nervous laugh. "Why do you like me? I have all these kids . . . I was a jerk to you . . . I'm perplexed."

A grin peeked out from the corner of his lips as he looked over at me and shook his head. "That right there. You don't even know how beautiful of a woman you are. If you knew, it'd take away part of the beauty about you. You see, I've seen you load those kids up and go to church every Sunday with nobody making you. I see you going to work and living life the way you do with your girls. You're a beautiful human being, and I know you might be a little rough around the edges, but I don't care. You were shaped, you were made, you were created by God, and I see Him when I look at you and your life."

His words strummed the strings of my heart as they fell from his lips. They invigorated my soul and made me feel beautiful. "You don't realize how much I loved hearing you say those words! But we have to take it slow for now. Be friends. You know? To a degree . . . hope that makes sense?"

He nodded. "I get it. Could I take you and the girls out boating Saturday? There's a great little spot not many people know about where I'd love to take you all."

"I'm sure the girls would love that, and I would too." His ability to respect my boundaries filled me with a deep sense of love. I knew it wasn't actual love, but it sure felt a lot like it. The idea of truly being in a relationship with him began to swirl my thoughts and tug at my heart, but with it came a bit of anxiety. I had been hurt so badly by Bradley, and giving my heart away to another man who could do the same scared me. After all, Bradley had been a great guy when I first met him. I knew I had praying to do, because a relationship didn't just mean me and him. My girls would be involved too, and I

didn't want them to get attached to someone just to

see him fade away like their father did.

CHAPTER 11

Saturday, the girls and I ventured over to Dylan's house after breakfast. As we came up to the dock at Dylan's, we could see him loading a cooler into the back of his boat. My girls, Bailey and Tristan, both had life vests on, and Emily had her backpack full of the needed supplies for the trip, and under one of my arms I carried an armful of towels.

Dylan stood up in the boat as he heard us step onto the dock. With no shirt on and his muscles bulging, I couldn't help but drink him in with my eyes like an ice cold glass of water. Cupping his hand over his eyes, he smiled. "You girls ready for a fun day out on the water?"

Bailey began to skip as we made our way down to

the boat. "I want to see where mermaids live!" she exclaimed.

"Mermaids aren't real," Emily added.

Dylan laughed. "You don't know that, Emily." Looking over at Bailey, he continued. "They *could* be real. You don't know unless you look."

"Mako Island mermaids live in a cave," Bailey informed Dylan, lifting her chin as she climbed into the boat.

"That's a TV show, not real life," Emily added.

"Well, we aren't going to a cave, but *maybe* we'll see one," Dylan said, causing Bailey's eyes to go wide with excitement. I loved the fact that Dylan was playing along with Bailey about the mermaids.

Tristan chimed in. "The Mako Island mermaids just

visit the cave. They don't live there."

Climbing into the boat after the girls, Dylan grabbed my hand to help me in, and I smiled as he led me over to the seat next to his. I grabbed for Emily's backpack she had set down behind me. As I pulled it to me, the boat rocked a little from the waves and it suddenly took my mind back to my younger days and being on the water. My friends and I were like fish during the summer—always swimming. Pulling out a water bottle, I took a long drink to relieve my thirst and try to push my attention away from Dylan's gorgeous body. It might have only been ten in the morning, but it was already quite warm.

Soon, we were full-speed ahead and cruising across the lake like a rock being skipped across the water. The wind tossed my hair back behind me and made me feel free as we bumped along the wavy water.

Glancing over my shoulder as I saw our houses get smaller, I felt free from the chaos and demands of my life.

Rounding the corner further up the lake, the houses disappeared entirely and I turned my head to look at Dylan. He was standing tall and kept a straight eye ahead on the water, swerving when needed to dodge random pieces of wood in the water. His shades on and the moisture of the water spray glistening against his body made me feel like I was in some kind of heaven. He turned to me and shouted over the sound of the boat. "You look gorgeous today, Charlotte."

I smiled as the compliment warmed me. He knew just what to say to make a woman feel good about herself. He grinned and then continued paying attention to the waters ahead.

We slowed down as we came up to a small sandy shore that had no houses or walking access and sat at the base of a steep hill. Dylan shifted the boat to idle and Bailey glanced back from the front seat where she and Tristan were sitting. Emily was in the back of the boat behind me. Bailey's eyes were wide in wonderment as she said, "Mommy . . . the mermaids are here?"

I smiled at her.

Glancing over, I saw Dylan take off his shades and toss them below the windshield. I couldn't help but steal a glance of his perfect physique once more. Suddenly, a chuckle came from behind me. Jerking my head back, I saw Emily laughing. I knew she had caught my wandering eye, and I went red in embarrassment.

"I'm going to check for large rocks in the water so we can dock it without ruining my boat," Dylan said.

I gave him a confirming nod, and before I could say anything, he dove right over the side and swam away from the boat. As I watched him and each muscular arm lift out of the water, I felt a deepening desire for those arms to wrap themselves around me. Then a hand suddenly found my shoulder.

"Mom," Emily said, grinning as she sat down in the driver seat.

"What?"

"You *totally* dig Dylan. Don't you?"

Flush with embarrassment, I shook my head. "Absolutely not! And if I did, I wouldn't tell you. You're my daughter and I'm your mother. We don't talk about these kinds of things."

She raised an eyebrow of skepticism.

"Stop it!"

Emily smiled and let out a laugh so electric that I could hardly believe it. I hadn't seen her have this much fun in a long time. I couldn't help but join in with the laugh as she started singing, 'Dylan and Mom sitting in a tree, K-I-S-S-I-N-G.'

After the laughter stopped, I looked at her and framed her face in my palm. "You really shouldn't worry yourself about these kinds of things, Emily. I'm a grown woman and you're my daughter." I put a hand on her shoulder. "I'm serious, Emily."

"I'm not a kid anymore, Mom. I get you and Dylan." Emily's eyes went over to the water. "He's cute. You two would make a cute couple, and it's been nice seeing you so happy lately."

Shaking my head, I said, "I have enough to worry about with you girls. I don't think things will really go anywhere with this guy."

"You have to take care of yourself too, Mom!" Emily retorted. I felt our conversation quickly growing inappropriate.

"I know. Thank you for the concern, Emily." Standing up, I took the backpack up to the front with me and gave Tristan and Bailey animal crackers for a quick treat and an easy diversion from the conversation with Emily. Glancing back at her, I saw she was still smiling and looking at me. I returned the smile and then doled out more cookies to the younger girls.

A few moments later, Dylan swam back to the boat.

"Charlotte!" he called out.

Coming over to the edge of the boat, I raised my eyebrows, "What?"

"Bring the boat over here." He pointed over to further down the shore. "And Emily, toss the flag up so people know we're in the water. Also, toss the buoys over the left side."

"Got it!" Emily replied, heading over to the left side of the boat as I headed to the driver's seat.

With one hand on the wheel and one on the throttle, I put it into a low speed and began to come in closer to the shore. Dylan swam up to the side and climbed over into the boat. Water poured off him and onto the floor of the boat. Coming up to me, he placed his dripping hands on both my arms and gently moved me to the side. The strength in his hands was there, but the gentleness he used as he touched me warmed the fire that was already burning inside me. There was just something about a man with strength using gentleness that made me swoon. Stepping out of the way, I watched as the water slid down his spine.

Glancing back at me, he said, "Tie the rope onto that rock right there." He pointed over to an oddly shaped rock that stuck out from the water.

Once I finished tying the rope to the rock he suggested, he stood up. "All right. We're good!" Dylan clapped and shut off the boat. Jumping over the boat, we all followed him into the water and over to the shore.

"This place is cool," Emily said as we all walked out onto the shore. She went over to a giant piece of drift wood and sat down. Wringing her ponytail out, she looked over at me. "Have you ever been here?"

I shook my head as I turned to see Bailey and Tristan scurry down the shoreline. "Been to some neat places around here like the Jackson's Bayou but never this place."

Dylan nodded. "Jackson's is cool. We used to boat down there for lunch a bunch when I was a kid." His eyes ran along the shore down where Bailey and Tristan were. They turned and started back our direction. "This place has been one of my favorites forever. I recall many summers coming to visit my family in Newport and coming right here to this spot." Dylan and I sat down on a log as Bailey and Tristan came back over and sat down in the sand.

Dylan began to tell a story to the girls about three sisters who were mermaids. I was captivated as I watched my sweet Bailey hang from every word he uttered. Tristan was right there with her, and I even caught a glimpse of Emily smiling. My girls were having a good time with a man who wasn't their father. It was a first for them, and it warmed my soul.

As I looked at Dylan, I could sense his sincerity. He wasn't doing it to impress me. He was genuinely enjoying himself. Maybe all my *baggage* wasn't really 'baggage' to the right guy.

After swimming and a few more stories, we took the boat back to Dylan's dock and he fired up the barbecue while I ran over to my house to grab burgers and buns. As I opened up the fridge and searched for the condiments, I heard my phone buzz on the counter, but I ignored it. I didn't care who it was. I was where I wanted to be and with whom I wanted to be. Whoever it was could wait.

Returning back over to Dylan's, the girls weren't out on the back porch. I knew Emily had already left to go over to her friend's house, but Bailey and Tristan should have been there. "Where are the girls?" I asked as I came over and handed him the burgers and set down the rest of the supplies on the picnic table.

"They went inside to play with some of the toys I pulled out that were Jenny's."

I nodded. "Oh . . ."

He turned to me as he finished putting the patties on the grill. "What? Jenny's toys? Don't worry about it. I'm okay."

"But the other night, you—"

He interrupted. "I know. It was just the anniversary—always a hard day. I'm fine with the girls playing with the toys. Don't worry about it." He shut the grill hood and stepped over to me. Brushing my hair behind my ear, his eyes lingered on my face and then directly into my eyes. I could feel his soul touch mine as he smoothed his thumb against my cheek. Leaning in, he looked deeper into my eyes.

He pulled back.

"What? What's wrong?" I asked, touching his arm.

He shook his head. "You wanted to go slow. I'm sorry." He went over to the picnic table and grabbed the cheese and seasoning.

As he walked back to the grill, I grabbed his arm and pulled him to me. Framing his face with my hands, I pressed up on my tiptoes and kissed him. He dropped the cheese and seasoning, then grabbed onto my waist as he kissed me with a passion that consumed me like a wildfire. My insides melted, and as our kiss deepened, he paused and nibbled on my lip, causing my knees to give way.

A whisper in my mind told me to stop, but I ignored it. Dylan must have had the same whisper as he slowly and grudgingly unlocked his lips from mine and set me back arm-length distance. Taking a deep breath and letting it out, he said, "I need to be careful. *We* need to be careful." Slowly, he leaned down to pick up the cheese and seasoning.

Pressing my hand against my forehead as I nodded, I replied, "I know."

He continued over to the grill and set the stuff down. Pausing, he glanced back at me and gave me a look like he just wanted to scoop me up in his arms and kiss me. I stepped toward him as he pulled me into his arms and began to kiss me again. Pausing as his lips were less than an inch away from mine, he said, "You're intoxicating. I can't get enough of you." We continued to kiss.

Slowly realizing how quickly things were escalating, I pulled back. "Mmm." Grudgingly, I said, "We must behave, Dylan." Taking a step back, I had the control this time. "Those burgers are going to burn."

He nodded and returned back to the barbecue. Watching as he finished up the burgers, I saw a man who was more than anything I could have prayed

for. He was passionate, strong, emotional, and a

man who respected my boundaries.

CHAPTER 12

As I was walking downstairs from tucking Bailey and Tristan into bed, I smiled. The cavern, the swimming, the barbeque . . . it was all so perfect. Dylan was perfect. Walking through the living room, I could see him through the open doorway. He began to build a fire out in the fireplace. Going over to the stove, I pulled the kettle off the burner and filled it with water for tea. I set it on the burner and began to make some coffee for him when suddenly, my phone began to buzz over on the counter.

Recalling it had gone off earlier, I decided to see who it was.

It was Edith.

I answered. "Hello?"

"Good! You finally answered! I've been trying to reach you all day, Charlotte!"

"Oh, sorry. I've been out on the water all day and then at a barbeque next door."

"With *Dylan*?" she questioned.

"Yes. How do you know him?"

"He's an Atkin, Charlotte!" Edith scolded.

I walked over to the doorway and looked at Dylan as he turned around at the fireplace. Staring into his gorgeous brown eyes, I said, "I know that, Edith . . . and I'm just done caring about the feud. Dylan is good, I promise."

"Hm." I could tell by her tone that she wasn't thrilled to hear that bit of information, but I didn't care. I wasn't going to lose him again. I almost lost him forever because of the silly feud.

"I think it's time to put it all behind us. It happened *so* long ago."

Edith let out a sigh. I thought for a second she was coming to her senses, but I was wrong. "Easy for you to say, Charlotte. It's not *your* family!" She paused and waited for a response, but continued when I didn't give her one. "You'd better be careful with that Atkin boy! You don't know what they're capable of doing."

"Um. Yes, I do know what they're capable of doing. Dylan's not like that. He's different. And shouldn't we, as Christians, be rising above this silly feud anyway?"

A deep sigh came from the other end of the phone. "Be careful, Charlotte."

importantly, a man of God."

Letting out a sigh, I let down my defenses. "It's true. But there's a part of me that is scared of him."

"Why on earth would *he* scare you?" my mother asked as she finished her drink of iced tea.

I tilted my head slightly without saying a word and looked at her.

"You can't let what happened with Bradley hold you back in your life, Charlotte. Don't let that jerk have control over you."

My eyes drifted back to the yard where the girls and Dylan were playing. "You don't care about him being an Atkin?"

My mother laughed. "I love Edith and her family dearly, but I wouldn't ever hold someone's name against them. That would be preposterous. I am glad you finally came to your senses."

Emily let out a laugh and twirled in the grass as Bailey ran circles around her. I felt a soul stirring warm settle into me. Dylan made sense. For me, my girls and for my life. He was everything I ever wanted, and he made me feel loved the way I had always wanted to be loved. He made me feel beautiful.

Bailey and Tristan were exhausted later that afternoon and wanted a movie on upstairs before I left to take my mother home. After putting the movie on, I went to leave, but Tristan called out to me. "Mom?"

"Yes, dear?" I asked at the doorway, looking back at her.

"Are you and Dylan going to get married?"

Warmth wrapped itself around my heart at the thought, but I quickly pushed it aside for logic. What the future held for Dylan and me was unclear, and my girls didn't need to worry about any such matter. Their thoughts needed to be on mermaids and far off princesses and castles, not if their mother was going to marry the next door neighbor. "We're just friends, dear."

"But don't you like him, Mom?" Tristan pressed.

"Well, *yeah*."

Tristan shrugged. "Why don't you marry him then?"

"Mommy, you should marry him!" Bailey added.

With a laugh in my voice I said, "We're not talking about this, girls. Enjoy the movie!"

Shutting their door, I shook my head as I smiled. *Children.* I headed back downstairs and found Emily on the couch with ear buds in and a sketch pad on her lap. As I walked into the living room, she pulled the ear buds out. "Hey, Mom."

"Hey."

"Could I go with Ashley and Brianna to *The Newport Theater*'s opening next week?"

"Yeah. I can give you guys a ride to it." Glancing back at the stairs, I said, "Your sisters are watching a movie upstairs. Keep an ear out for them, please. I'm taking Grandma home."

"Thanks, and will do." Smiling, Emily put her ear buds back in and went back to her sketch pad.

Walking to the car, I saw my mother already in the passenger seat. She was sitting quietly, reading one of her western romance novels as I came up to the car. Her love for westerns stemmed from her deep love of cowboys. My father often took her horseback riding when they were a young couple. I flashed her a grin as I got into the car. "What number is that for the month?"

"Oh, stop pestering me!" she retorted, placing a bookmark in to save her spot. Placing the book in her purse, she continued, "The sermon Pastor gave today was nice."

I nodded. "Edith was giving me dagger eyes the

whole time during service." Letting out a sigh, I continued, "She's upset Dylan and I are friends."

"*Friends?* Is that what you're calling it?"

I put the car into reverse and began to back out of the driveway. "It's a friendship for now, Mother."

She crossed her hands together in her lap and shook her head. "I don't know why you young people waste so much time in life! Your father and I were married at nineteen, and I spent many years with him . . . but it didn't seem like enough."

"I'm thirty-seven. I'm not exactly young. You're right about you and Dad not wasting any time . . . but it's different for me. I have my girls to look after." Turning onto her street, we came to a stop in front of her house.

Opening the door, she paused and looked over at

me. "Don't waste your life away waiting, or you'll miss your chance with Dylan."

"Okay, mother," I replied with a smile.

She closed the door, and I turned around in the middle of the street to head back home. As I drove, I thought about Dylan and how much I wanted to be with him. I was scared, but I was so ready to be in those arms of his in a more permanent sense. *He's good with the girls.* I nodded. *He's a good kisser.* I nodded again. *He likes spending time with me.* I smiled. *He's godly.* There was no reason to not be with him. Fear couldn't hold me back any longer.

Pulling back into my driveway, I saw two trucks, one with a boat in tow, parked in Dylan's driveway. *That's a little odd.* Getting out, I crossed through the grass and over to Dylan's front door. Knocking, I waited for him to answer. Each second that passed filled me with more anticipation than the previous moment. When he opened the door, I could see Frank and Cody sitting in his living room. My pulse began to race.

"Hey, Charlotte." He held onto the door. "What's up?"

Shaking my head, I stepped back. "Nothing."

"What?" He shook his head and grinned. "You knocked on my door for nothing?"

A couple of quick shakes of my head, and I said, "I'll talk to you later." Turning, I darted back across the lawn as my heart pounded. Seeing Frank and Cody gave me a bad feeling. Was he telling them about the part of the paddle we found? I prayed not, but I had no way of knowing.

At four o'clock, while I was doing the dishes, I saw the brothers emerge from the house through my kitchen window. Frank and Cody left in their trucks, but Dylan strolled down his driveway toward the back. Placing the last plate in the dishwasher I went out to my patio to watch him. He traveled down to the dock, then got into his boat and seemed to search around for something.

"Mommy!" Bailey shouted from behind me, startling me.

"Yes?" I replied whipping around. "What is it, Bailey?"

"Can I have a hug? I missed you!" She rubbed an eye as she stepped closer to me. Bending down, I pulled her into my arms and kissed her cheek. "Did you fall asleep watching your movie?"

She nodded.

A knock came from the back door.

Opening the door, Dylan smiled. "Sorry about earlier. I didn't expect them. It was a random thing with Cody and Frank stopping by."

Shrugging it off, I said, "No need to apologize. It's your family."

He squinted at me. "I know how you feel about *them*. Anyhow, what brought you over that you didn't want to talk about in front of them?"

A few quick shakes of my head to dismiss the visit didn't suffice him. He pressed again.

I replied, "Look—just drop it. Okay?"

Bailey scurried out of the room and upstairs. Dylan saw her going upstairs and stepped into the kitchen, closing the door behind him. Our eyes connected as he reached to draw me to him. "I like you, Charlotte. My heart's desire is to be with you." His eyebrows went up. "I can't stop thinking about that kiss."

Smiling as I revisited the moment, I nodded in acknowledgement. "Me too."

He drew me closer and gently drew my hands toward his lips. His touch drove me crazy. "Why can't we have that? I promise I won't ever hurt you. I understand your ex hurt you badly . . . but I'm not him. I'm not like that." Gently caressing his lips to my fingertips, he said, "Please give me a chance, Charlotte."

My heart pounded as Dylan serenaded me with his sweet words. It took everything within me not to fall into his arms right then, right there in the middle of my kitchen. "Dylan, I'm just scared. Wanting to be with you was actually why I went to your house earlier . . . I feel the same way you do."

Bringing me in close to him, he said, "You don't need to worry." Softly, with the tips of his fingers, he brushed my hair behind my ear and let his fingers glide against my skin, down my neck, sending my heart into overdrive with emotion. "I'm crazy about you, Charlotte. My soul feels drawn to you." His lips came to my neck, where his fingers had just traced. Feeling his breath against my skin caused my breathing to quicken. Then his lips pressed against my neck as he slowly kissed his way up to my earlobe, causing my knees to weaken.

"Mom," Emily's voice from the couch in the other room echoed through my skull from behind me. Dylan let go of me and we quickly separated.

Pushing aside my annoyance for being interrupted, I replied from the kitchen, "Yes?"

"What's for dinner?"

"Steak. And Dylan's cooking it." I raised my eyebrows at Dylan.

He grinned and nodded.

"Cool."

Stepping closer to Dylan, I grabbed his hand and kissed the inside of his palm. Bring it up to my cheek, I pressed it against my skin. I closed my eyes for a moment and then opened them to look into his eyes. "Don't hurt me, Dylan. Because when you hurt me, you hurt my girls, and they don't deserve anymore pain in life."

"I promise I won't. Hey—I have something for you."

My interest was piqued. "Yeah?"

"Wait right here."

"Okay," I replied as I watched him head out the door.

Returning a few minutes later with heavy breaths, he held a hand behind his back. "Sorry. I didn't want to keep you waiting."

I laughed. "It's fine. What is it?"

He composed himself and pulled his hand from behind his back to reveal a beautifully carved Blue Jay on a perch. "I carved it the other day when I couldn't stop thinking about you. I want you to have it."

Taking the bird in my hand, I smoothed my thumb over it and admired the intricate details he had put into it. "You carved this while you were thinking about me?"

He nodded.

Smiling, I looked at him and said, "Thank you."

"You're welcome." He came closer and brought my chin up, connecting his eyes with mine. "I promise never to hurt you, Charlotte."

CHAPTER 14

The Newport Theater's grand re-opening was soon upon us one Saturday Evening. Anybody who was somebody in Newport would be in attendance for the event. Serenah even shut down the Bed and Breakfast for the event. The night's event was formal, and that meant the girls and I were all dressed up for the seven o'clock ribbon cutting that would be taking place on the red carpet just outside the front entrance to the theater. I was sporting a black cocktail dress, had my hair up in a French twist, and my bangs were curled to each side. It was the first time in a long time that I felt beautiful.

"You look great, Mom!" Emily said from my bedroom doorway as I stood in front of my full-sized mirror near the dresser in my room. Whipping around, I saw that she was wearing her new dress she had picked out from one of the local shops downtown just a few days ago when we were all out on an outing with Dylan. The dress was more than I wanted to spend, but I knew it was worth it. She was excited about the evening, and probably even more so than me since Jake Gillian was going to be there. He was a boy from her high school who had been coming over to the house for a summer study program.

"You look like a beautiful young woman, my Emily," I replied.

She beamed with a smile and headed back downstairs to her friends, Ashley and Brianna, who were dropped off by their parents earlier in the day. As I put my earrings on, a picture next to the bird

Dylan had carved for me on the dresser caught my eye. It was a family picture of when Bradley and I took the girls to visit New York City. In that photo, he had a fake, forced smile that he seemed to carry on all our family outings. He had almost always been on his phone between photographs, obsessing over the latest trends and figures coming out of Wall Street. He was always looking to the future, yet never able to enjoy the present. He thought he could just throw money and fix everything that way— including his dislikes with me. I hated to draw comparisons, but I couldn't help it. Dylan was nothing like him, and I was so thankful for that.

Joining Emily and the girls downstairs, we girls all made our way out to the car.

As we arrived at *The Newport Theater* a few minutes later, I was surprised by how many blocks we had to drive to find a spot to park. As we got out of the car and headed down the sidewalk, we all watched as the spotlights danced across the overcast clouds that looked to be loaded with rain that could fall any minute.

"They look like they're chasing each other, huh?" I said over to the girls.

Tristan said, "Yeah. They're so cool looking!"

I nodded and kept my eyes fixed ahead down the sidewalk in search for Dylan in the crowd that was forming around the red carpet out front of *The Newport Theater*. I knew he was there, but I just didn't know where.

Seeing Serenah and Charlie we stopped to say hello.

"Could I talk to you?" Serenah asked, tilting her head to the side.

"Sure," I replied. We walked a few steps away to the side of the building.

"Would you be in my wedding? As a bridesmaid?" she asked, her eyebrows raised and a smile I couldn't resist.

"I'd love to do that for you."

Serenah let out a relieving sigh and touched my arm. "Thank goodness. I was worried you might not agree to on such short notice. I just don't . . . have a lot of people in town."

I smiled. "I'm happy to be there for you. Thank you."

Charlie took Serenah by the hand and they vanished into the crowd while I returned to pursue Dylan. A few people shifted their steps out of the way and suddenly Dylan came into view. He looked absolutely breathtaking in his tuxedo. I could have sworn that man grew more handsome every time I saw him. He turned his head and our eyes met. I hurried my steps the rest of the way to meet him.

"Charlotte," Dylan said from across the rope that separated the carpet from the sidewalk.

"I know we're a little late, but we did have to walk a bit. I tried my best to get here on time."

He nodded but didn't seem to care about the lateness. He scanned all of us and a grin came across his face. "You all look like a bunch of beautiful princesses." He connected with my eyes again. "And of course, the gorgeous *queen*." Leaning in across the rope, he raised my chin up with his finger and kissed me on the lips in front of everybody. Flashes from the photographers were blinding.

"Dylan!" a man said from behind him as we pulled

away from the kiss.

Turning around, Dylan started talking with the man. He stopped, though, and leaned back to me, gently kissing me on my lips. "I'll see you inside." He turned and went with the man, talking to him as he vanished beyond my sight. My phone rang—it was Edith.

"Hello?" I answered, stepping away from the girls and the crowd further down the sidewalk.

"Just wanted to let you know you have a couple of Atkin brothers on a boat out in the water near your house."

My world began to crumble around me. "Um."

"Um?" Edith replied hotly. "What's going on? What aren't you telling me? You know something I don't."

"Um . . ." My mind was racing as my heart felt like it was being stabbed repeatedly, and 'um' was all I could come up with in the moment. *He's a good guy. Dylan wouldn't betray me.* Almost able to grab onto hope, I was shot down by another thought. *You thought Bradley was a good guy too.*

"Quit saying 'um' and speak, woman!" Edith fired back.

"He wasn't supposed to tell anyone. Dylan said he didn't care about any of this."

"Tell anyone what?"

"We found a piece of the raft's paddle on the shore that had the town crest on it."

Edith shouted, "You trusted an Atkin boy! I warned you, Charlotte! I warned you!"

Click.

She hung up.

Hurrying back over to the crowd, I pushed past people in search of Dylan. Then I saw him lean in and shake the hand of Cody and pat him on the shoulder. With tear-filled eyes, I shook my head. He looked over at me, startled. *It's true.* Turning, I headed back out of the crowd. Wiping the tears from my eyes, I maintained. Stopping at my girls, I said, "Something came up. I'll be back to pick you up. I love you." Kissing their heads, I stopped at Emily. "Keep an eye on your sisters."

She nodded. "What's wrong, Mom?"

Shaking my head as my heart pounded and my throat felt like it was tightening, I replied, "I'm fine." Continuing onward to my car, I let my emotions of betrayal, loss, and sadness fuel my heels as they clanked against the sidewalk and tears fell from my eyes.

CHAPTER 15

Back at my house, I found that what Edith said was true. The Atkin brothers' boat I had seen in Dylan's driveway the other day was now out on the lake. The shred of hope I managed to cling to on my way home evaporated in an instance. Everything I felt for Dylan was built on trust and honesty, which was now eroding away.

Hurrying across my property and down to Dylan's dock, I made my way to his boat. Climbing in, I turned the key and fired it up. There was a break in the clouds above, and the moonlight shone down across the lake. Under different circumstances, I would have found it beautiful, but right now, I found it meaningless.

As I pulled away from the dock, I heard a car pull up. Glancing back, I saw Dylan running down the driveway to the dock. "Charlotte!" he shouted as I headed further out. I glanced over my shoulder at him again but ignored his plea.

Arriving at the Atkins' boat, I shouted over the edge as I turned off my motor. "Show yourself! I know you're in that boat, Frank!"

Silence returned.

Getting comfortable in my seat, I waited for Frank to surface as I suspected he must have gone diving. I ignored the faint sounds from the shoreline where Dylan stood in his tuxedo, yelling. I laughed as I felt raindrops begin to fall. Peering back across the lake, I saw Dylan continue to stand there in his three-hundred-dollar tuxedo and ruin it in the rain. *Idiot.*

Turning my eyes to heaven as it began raining, I cried out to the Lord. "Why must I pick such horrible men? Please help me to just be in love with You for the rest of my life. I'm weary of these games of the heart." I began crying. "Help me be strong for my girls! I can't do it without You, God!"

Suddenly, a splash came from between my boat and the other boat. Jumping up, I saw Frank emerge. A look of fear as he laid eyes on me came across his face. "What are you doing here?" he asked.

"What are *you* doing here? This is private property, and you know by law you're not permitted to be here."

"Thought you'd be at *The Newport Theater* tonight."

I furrowed my eyebrows as he pulled off his goggles. "Get in your boat and get out of here."

"Nothing down there anyway," Frank replied, climbing up the back of his boat.

"Cool! I don't care!"

He took off back to shore and loaded his boat, but I noticed Dylan didn't help him. As I drove back to the shoreline after watching him leave, I shook my head as I saw Dylan *still* standing in the rain in his tuxedo. I arrived back at the dock, and Dylan came down and helped tie it up. Climbing out of the boat and standing up on the dock, I faced him.

He grabbed my hand but I pulled away. "Charlotte, you have to hear me out." He followed me as I walked away down the dock. Stopping, I turned to him.

"You told them, Dylan!" I held out my hand toward the lake. My eyes watered and my lip trembled. "You told them about the paddle." Shaking my head, I continued. "After all that talk about how earthly treasure doesn't matter to you." I turned and began down the dock again, but he grabbed my arm. He pulled me back and looked me in the eyes as the rain became a downpour.

"They found the piece of paddle you gave me and pressed for the information!"

I shook my head. "You should have kept your mouth shut!"

Shaking his head, he replied, "They helped me get a new start. They bought *The Newport Theater* for me."

"So what? You told them to go dive in the lake tonight when you had me off at *The Newport Theater*? That's messed up! You went behind my back, *Dylan!*" I smacked him in the chest. "I trusted you!"

Water poured down his face as the rain continued. He shook his head. "I told them *never* to set foot in this lake! I protected you and the Townsons the best I could!"

"You never cared about the Townsons, Dylan— admit it." I turned to leave again, and he grabbed my arm. He pulled me into his arms and grabbed my face, kissing me passionately. Startled, I pushed him back off me and slapped him. This time, when I turned to leave, he didn't stop me.

I drove to *The Newport Theater* and called my mother to explain what had happened while I waited for the movie to end. She went on and on about how no one is perfect and everyone makes mistakes, no matter what family they're associated with, and then she said something that struck me deeply.

"What would Jesus want you to do in regards to Dylan?"

Anger boiled inside me. "Mom! He never told me that they knew!"

"So?" A long, drawn sigh came from my mother's lips on the other end of the phone. "It doesn't matter. Dylan's flawed."

"Well . . . I thought he was perfect."

"A perfect man or person doesn't exist unless you read books like I do. You have to find someone you can love and make it work with them!"

Looking up, I saw Dylan walking into *The Newport Theater* with his drenched tuxedo, slouching his shoulders and hanging his head. He might have not been perfect, but he was perfect for me. I still believed it. I was just mad. I knew I had to get over this and realize he did everything he could in the situation he was put in. "I'm going to try and make it right, Mom."

Getting off the phone, I tossed it onto the seat beside me and got out. Hurrying through the pouring rain down the sidewalk and into the theater, I got inside and past the ticket takers.

Walking into the lobby area, I was overwhelmed with surprise—not by Dylan, but by the work he had done on *The Newport Theater*. The inside that he had redone paid tribute to the town of Newport more than I could have ever dreamed. Included was a family mural of the Townsons and the Atkins. As I looked beyond the family murals and to the other walls, my smile grew as I saw a giant blue jay and the view from my patio with the fireplace—even the stars and the moonlit lake view were all painted on one of the walls. My eyes began to well with tears, and then a hand touched my shoulder.

Turning around, Dylan was standing there, still in his drenched tuxedo and water dripping from the tips of his hair. "I'm so sorry, Charlotte—"

Interrupting him, I stepped closer and grabbed his face, pulling him into me and planting my lips on his. He grinned and brought his palm up, cupping my cheek in his hand, deepening the kiss as the warmth of love coursed through me. Though the theater let out a moment later, we continued to kiss as if we were stuck in that moment forever. Placing a hand on my back, he brought me to his chest.

From that night on, I let go of every petty thing and let God be God in my life. Disregarding my fears and insecurities, I was able to truly love and be loved. That night, I didn't say 'I do' at an altar like I did years ago with Bradley, but instead, I made the choice to say 'I will.' *I will* to life, *I will* to the ups and downs, and *I will* to the life God had given to me. God had remade me and given me a new beginning one Saturday evening.

The End.

One Saturday Evening

Did you enjoy the Book?

Please
Leave a Review

BOOK PREVIEW

Preview of "Amongst the Flames"

Prologue

Fire. Four letters, two vowels and one reaction.

That reaction depends on who you are. For me and the fellas at Station 9 in downtown Spokane, our reaction is one of quickness, speed and precision. A few seconds delay could mean someone's life. We don't have time to think, only do. And we don't do this for the recognition or because it's just some job, we do it because this is what we were born to do. My resume, if I had one, would only say one thing on it: Firefighter. I'm one of those guys that you don't really think about unless something has gone terribly wrong. Usually it's when your house is on fire.

I won't bore you with the countless calls where we just show up with our lights on and we're just there to support the police and ambulance. I'm sure you've seen us sitting across the street quietly once or twice while they wheel Mrs. Johnson out on a gurney to the ambulance at three o'clock in the morning. I also won't explain to you the hundred calls a year we get on burning popcorn in a kitchen. No. This story I'm going to share with you is not only about the worst fire I had ever seen in my life, but it'll also encompass how important God is, not only in marriage, but in life.

This is not a story you'll find on the front page of your local newspaper while you're sipping your morning cup of coffee. You also won't catch it on the ten o'clock news. Nope. Instead, it's a story that will inspire you to look at life differently and challenge you to believe that with God even the worst fire you face is nothing in comparison with His power, grace and mercy.

Belief in God is not really an option for me when I run into burning buildings to save lives. It's a core fundamental building block of who I am. I won't sit here and tell you that I'm a perfect Christian though; that would be a lie. Soon enough, you'll read about my plethora of issues and flaws amongst the pages that follow. What I will do is stay true to the truth the best that I can. I'm not telling this story to make a record of my sins or those of others. I'm giving you this story to give you hope. Hope of a brighter tomorrow that you can look forward to, hope of a world where acceptance isn't only preached, but it's applied alongside the scriptures to our lives.

I am Cole Taylor and this is my story.

Chapter 1

Walking down an aisle in the grocery store with

Kane, Micah and Greg one morning at about eight

o'clock I couldn't help but laugh a little. I caught

Kane checking out a pretty brunette a few aisles over

in the bakery.

"Always on the prowl, aren't ya?" I asked, smiling

over at him. Kane was the station's notorious single

twenty-three-year-old male with nothing but

women on his mind. He once admitted to me that

he bought a full set of turnouts online from an ex-

fireman just so he could suit up in a full fireman

outfit for a girl.

"She's cute," Kane replied with a half-grin on his

face. He shot another look over at her and his smile

grew.

"Maybe she can bake you a cake or something?"
Greg said with a soft but sarcastic tone as he
grabbed a box of pasta from the shelf. Greg was one
of the quieter guys on the crew.

Micah and I erupted in laughter. Kane smiled and
said, "I'm sure there's more to her than that."

"How would you even know that?" I asked.

He shrugged. "It's a hunch, I know about these
things."

"Well, at least you know she has a sweet side,"
Micah added. Kane laughed a little as he pushed the
cart down towards the end of the aisle.

On the way over to the meat section of the store, a
man with furrowed eyebrows made a beeline for us.
Leaning into Kane's ear, I said, "Move the cart out of
his way." Kane did, but it didn't help. The elderly

gentleman shifted his footing to line up with our cart as he continued towards us.

Arriving at us, the man latched his worn hands to each side of our cart and demanded in a sharp tone, "What are you doing here?"

"Same as most people here, just grocery shopping... you?" Kane asked, crossing his arms as he released his grip from the cart.

"Are you on the clock right now?" the man asked. He shot a quick look at each of us individually as if we were caught in some kind of predicament.

"Yeah," I replied, stepping in front of Kane and up to the gentleman. I knew I needed to get between them before Kane did something stupid. His fuse was short when it came to people who didn't respect firefighters. For instance, there was a call one time that Kane and I were on where the man whose house was on fire started complaining to us about how long it took us to respond. Kane took his revenge inside the home when he used the butt of his axe to smash the guy's big screen TV.

"Is there a problem going on in the store we should know about?" Micah asked, looking over my shoulder at the man. Micah was my best friend at the station and he was always looking for the best in people no matter what the situation appeared to be.

"Yeah, matter of fact there is a problem ya chump! And I'm looking right at it," he shouted, raising his hands from the cart. I looked back at Kane as I knew the comment would set him off. Catching his gaze before he said anything, I could see Kane trying to keep his mouth shut. That little stunt he pulled at that fire by smashing the guy's TV landed him with a suspension without pay.

Micah raised his hands. "We're just trying to get to some supplies, Sir."

"Yeah– he's right. We don't want any trouble, Sir. We need to keep moving." I grabbed onto the cart and began walking past the disgruntled citizen.

"This is how my tax dollars is spent, huh?" He asked as he laughed sarcastically, shaking his head at us.

"I'm filing a complaint with your station!" he said from behind us. He must have been looking at the back of our fleece pullovers as he continued, "Station 9... Who's in charge over there?"

"Thomas Sherwood and Sean Hinley are our Captains and Paul Jensen's the Chief," I said over my shoulder to him.

"I'll be calling them right away!" he shouted.

We all three managed to keep our cool and made it over to the meats. As we came up to the bunker with steaks and stopped, Kane said, "We risk our lives, yet people still find a reason to complain... What is with that?" He glanced back at the angry man as he now appeared to be arguing with a grocery store worker.

I turned to Kane. "Do you do this job because you want people to think you're a hero?"

"No..." he replied softly. "But that kind of thing just isn't right."

"No, it's not right," I agreed. "But we don't do this to impress people, Kane. You know that. We do this job because it's our duty and we do it to protect the people of Spokane. We serve them, no matter how poorly we get treated."

"Cole's right, man," Micah said with a nod. "We can't let people like him get in our head."

"We can't let them undermine our reasons for doing

this," Greg added.

"I find honor in what we do and someone like that just bugs me."

"I know it does," I replied, putting a hand on his shoulder. "And thank you for not saying anything to him." I turned back to the steaks. "What cut do we want boys?" I asked.

Suddenly dispatch came over all our radios for a fire at the Canyon Creek Apartments on South Westcliff. We all four began sprinting for the front doors. My heart began pounding as adrenaline coursed through every one of my veins. Weaving between the aisles and shopping carts, we made our way outside. Spotting a cart boy on the way through the parking lot, I stopped and told him about our cart in the back of the store. He thanked me and I headed over to the truck.

Micah jumped into the driver seat. He was the ladder company's engineer and that meant the man behind the wheel. Greg sat up front with Micah; his role varied and depended much on what was needed on each call. Kane and I were the guys who did search and rescue, cut power and helped with ventilation cuts on the roof.

As Kane and I suited up in the back, Kane asked, "Did you see that chick in the bakery look concerned as we dashed out of there?"

I laughed. "No, didn't catch that," I said, pulling up my suspenders across the front of my chest.

"When we go back later I'm going to go talk to her. Bet I can get those digits," he replied as he slid his Nomax head and neck protector over his eyes. "I'll for sure get her number."

"She could be married," I replied.

"Nah, I saw her left hand when she was putting out donuts in the window earlier."

I laughed. "Wait... what ever happened to that Heidi girl? I almost completely forgot about her."

"He got bored of her," Micah said over his shoulder to us. "He can't seem to stay interested in one gal; you know that."

"Shouldn't you be keeping your eyes on the road?" Kane retorted.

"Really though, man, what happened?" I asked, looking over at Kane.

"Just didn't work out," Kane said as he shrugged.

We slowed down as we arrived at the scene.

Glancing out my window, I could see the fire had already engulfed much of the apartment complex and I felt another surge of adrenaline. I was excited and yet terrified out of my mind of the unknown that lay before me. It was that way every time we got a call.

Glancing at the other fire truck on scene, I saw Thomas Sherwood, the shift captain of station 9 and my father-in-law. He was already on scene along with the other guys who rode over on the engine truck. They were already about done hooking up the hose to the hydrant as we came to a complete stop. Leaping from my seat, my feet barely hit the pavement before the captain reached me.

"We need a grab on the second floor," he shouted. "There's a four year old girl in apartment one-forty-two." My heart felt like it skipped a beat as I looked up at the roaring flames. Saving lives wasn't anything new for me, but I never could get used to it. Even after ten years of service, every time lives were at stake, it was difficult, especially when the lives of children were involved.

"Got it," I replied as I grabbed my oxygen tank from the side of the truck and secured it onto my back. Grabbing my axe and Halligan bar, I turned as I pulled my mask over my face and put on my helmet. A hand on my shoulder stopped me from heading directly to the building.

"And, Cole," the captain said as I turned around.

"Yeah?" I asked.

"Be careful in there, I don't have the energy to explain to my daughter how her husband died today."

"No worries, you haven't had to yet," I replied.

Turning, I looked at the apartment entrance and saw the black smoke billowing out the front door. I jogged up to the door and as I entered, I saw Rick, starting the exterior attack on the fire from outside with his hose in hand. He was spraying down the nearby building so it would not catch on fire. I gave him a nod. Rick Alderman was one of the veterans on the crew. It was he, Micah and I for the past ten years at fire station 9. Kane came on a couple years after me and the others all were fairly new, each under five years. The older vets from the old days when I first started —like Hillman and Conrad— moved away and transferred to other stations. But no matter who came or went, when we were on the scene we were like that of a brotherhood. No man left behind, ever.

Coming inside the burning building, I immediately noticed the extreme temperatures inside. It wasn't typical, a bit warmer than I was used to. I pushed the sensation of being trapped in a furnace out of my mind as I ventured in further. I trekked through the black smoke and up the stairs in search for the child. My jacket was failing to keep the high temperatures of the heat from my skin and the burning was digging in. Ignoring common-sense reactions to extreme situations is a requirement that they don't advertise in the job description. Who in his right mind after all would run into a burning building, on purpose?

My visibility was low at the top of the stairs inside. The charcoal-black smoke was thick and filled every square inch. Seeing a door within reach, I came up to it. Squinting, I could see it read 'one forty four.' It wasn't the one I needed. I trudged through the ever-thickening smoke as the heat gnawed at my skin until I found the apartment I needed. One-forty-two. Relieved, I grabbed for the door knob, but found it locked. Taking a few steps back, I launched a kick to the door that would have impressed an MMA fighter, but it wasn't enough to make it budge. I brought my Halligan front side and stuck it right between the door and the frame. My skin continued to burn from the heat and my muscles screamed in pain as I pried open the door. Finally, it budged open.

Stepping through the smoke filled room, I shouted, "Fire department, Call out!" The sound of the roaring flames and falling pieces of debris made it nearly impossible to hear anything else.

Lowering myself to the floor, I moved through the living room and reached a doorway. An explosion suddenly came from another part of the building. Covering my helmet, I braced myself for any falling debris. Continuing through the doorway and smoke, I noticed a smoldering teddy bear next to me. This must be the girl's room, I thought to myself as I raised my head to survey the room. Trying to see through the smoke was difficult, but I spotted a closet across the floor. I repeated, "Fire department, Call out!" as I inched my way over to the closet. Getting to the closet, I found the little girl almost about to lose consciousness. Ripping my mask off in a frenzy, I shoved it over her face and said, "It is going to be okay, I'm going to get you out of here." She struggled to breathe into the mask. Our breathing apparatuses weren't so easy to use when not properly trained. "Just try to take small and short breaths," I said.

I grabbed the little girl and held her close to my chest in my arms, using myself as a shield as I crawled back towards the doorway. Once back into the living room, I stood up for the rest of the journey out. But before I could reach the front door of the apartment, an explosion came from the kitchen. Covering the girl as much as possible and dropping to the floor, I protected her from the blast. But a piece of metal shot across the room from the explosion and hit me in the upper arm. I thanked God it was only my arm as I regained my footing and continued to the door with the girl. My adrenaline was pumping and my heart was pounding so hard that I had no idea how bad my wound was. As I came to the stairs that led out of the apartment, pain suddenly shot through my arm, sending me collapsing to the top of the stairs.

Lying there I turned my head and looked down to the base of the stairs. I could see through the mostly faded smoke as Kane came rushing through the doorway and up the stairs to me.

Did you enjoy this sample? Go to

<u>www.tkchapin.com</u> and get a copy today!

BOOK PREVIEW

Preview of "The Perfect Cast"

Prologue

Each of us has moments of impact in life. Sometimes it's in the form of *love*, and sometimes in the form of *sadness*. It is in these times that our world changes forever. They shape us, they define us, and they transform us from the people we once were into the people we now are.

The summer before my senior year of high school is one that will live with me forever. My parents' relationship was on the rocks, my brother was more annoying than ever, and I was forced to leave the world I loved and cared about in Seattle. A summer of change, a summer of growth, and a summer I'll never forget.

Chapter 1 ~ Jess

Jess leaned her head against the passenger side window as she stared out into the endless fields of wheat and corn. She felt like an alien in a foreign land, as it looked nothing like the comfort of her home back in Seattle.

She was convinced her friends were lucky to not have a mother who insisted on whisking them away to spend the *entirety* of their summer out in the middle of nowhere in Eastern Washington. She would have been fine with a weekend visit, but the entire summer at Grandpa's? That was a bit uncalled for, and downright wrong. Her mother said the trip was so Jess and her brother Henry could spend time with her grandpa Roy, but Jess had no interest in doing any such thing.

On the car ride to Grandpa's farm to be dropped off and abandoned, Jess became increasingly annoyed with her mother. Continually, her mother would glance over at Jess, looking for conversation. Ignoring her mom's attempts to make eye contact with her, Jess kept her eyes locked and staring out the window. Every minute, and every second of the car ride, Jess spent wishing the summer away.

After her mother took the exit off the freeway that led out to the farm, a loud pop came from the driver side tire and brought the car to a grinding halt. Her mom was flustered, and quickly got out of the car to investigate the damage. Henry, Jess's obnoxious and know-it-all ten-year-old brother, leaned between the seats and glanced out the windshield at their mom.

"Stop being so annoying," Jess said, pushing his face back between the seats. He sat back and then began to reach for the door. Jess looked back at him and asked, "What are you doing?"

"I'm going to help Mom."

"Ha. You can't help her; you don't know how to change a tire."

"Well, I am going to *try*." Henry climbed out of the car and shut it forcefully. Jess didn't want this summer to exist and it hadn't even yet begun. If only she could fast forward, and her senior year of high school could start, she'd be happy. But that wasn't the case; there was no remote control for her life. Instead, the next two and half months were going to consist of being stuck out on a smelly farm with Henry and her grandpa. She couldn't stand more than a few minutes with her brother, and being stuck in a house with no cable and *him*? That was a surefire sign that one of them wasn't making it home alive. Watching her mother stare blankly at the car, unsure of what to do, Jess laughed a little to herself. *If you wouldn't have left Dad, you would have avoided this predicament.* Her dad knew how to fix everything. Whether it was a flat tire, a problematic science project or her fishing pole, her dad was always there for her no matter what. That was up until her mother walked out on him, and screwed everybody's life up. He left out of the country on a three month hiatus. Jess figured he had a broken heart and just needed the time away to process her mom leaving him in the dust.

Henry stood outside the car next to his mother, looking intently at the tire. Accidentally catching eye contact with her mother, Jess rolled her eyes. Henry had been trying to take over as the *man of the house* ever since the split. It was cute at first, even to Jess, but his rule of male superiority became rather old quickly when Henry began telling Jess not to speak to her mother harshly and to pick up her dirty laundry. Taking the opportunity to cut into her mom, Jess rolled down her window. "Why don't you call Grandpa? Oh, that's right... he's probably outside and doesn't have a cell phone... but even if he did, he wouldn't have reception."

"Don't start with me, Jess." Her mother scowled at her. Jess watched as her mother turned away from the car and spotted a rickety, broken down general store just up the road.

Her mom began to walk along the side of the road with Henry. Jess didn't care that she wasn't invited on the family trek along the road. It was far too hot to walk anywhere, plus she preferred the coolness of the air conditioning. She wanted to enjoy the small luxury of air conditioning before getting to her grandpa's, where she knew there was sure to be nothing outside of box fans.

Jess pulled her pair of ear buds out from the front pouch of her backpack and plugged them into her phone. Tapping into her music as she put the ear buds in, she set the playlist to shuffle. Staring back out her window, she noticed a cow feeding on a pile of hay through the pine trees, just over the other side of a barbed wire fence. *I really am in the middle of nowhere.*

Chapter 2 ~ Roy

The blistering hot June sun shone brightly through the upper side of the barn and through the loft's open doorway, illuminating the dust and alfalfa particles that were floating around in the air. Sitting on a hay bale in the upper loft of the barn, Roy watched as his nineteen-year-old farmhand Levi retrieved each bale of hay from the conveyor that sat at the loft's doorway. Each bale of alfalfa weighed roughly ninety pounds; it was a bit heavier than the rest of the grass hay bales that were stored in the barn that year. Roy enjoyed watching his farmhand work. He felt that if he watched him enough, he might be able to rekindle some of the strength that he used to have in his youth.

While Roy was merely watching, that didn't

protect him from the loft's warmth, and sweat quickly began to bead on his forehead. Reaching for his handkerchief from his back pocket, he brought it to his forehead and dabbed the sweat. Roy appreciated the help of Levi for the past year. Whether it was feeding and watering the cattle, fixing fences out in the fields, or shooting the coyotes that would come down from the hill and attack the cows, Levi was always there and always helping. He was the son of Floyd Nortaggen, the man who ran the dairy farm just a few miles up the road. If it wasn't for Levi, Roy suspected he would have been forced to give up his farm and move into a retirement home. Roy knew retirement homes were places where people went to die, and he just wasn't ready to die. And he didn't want to die in a building full of people that he didn't know; he wanted to die out on his farm, where he always felt he belonged.

"Before too long, I'll need you to get up on the roof and get those shingles replaced. I'm afraid one good storm coming through this summer could ruin the hay."

Levi glanced up at the roof as he sat on the final bale of hay he had stacked. Wiping away the sweat from his brow with his sleeve, he looked over to Roy. "I'm sure I could do that. How old are the shingles?"

A deep smile set into Roy's face as he thought about when he and his father had built the barn back when he was just a boy. "It's been forty years now." His father had always taken a fancy to his older brother, but when his brother had gone away on a mission trip for the summer, his dad had relied on Roy for help with constructing the barn. Delighted, he'd spent the summer toiling in the heat with his dad. He helped lay the foundation, paint the barn and even helped put on the roof. Through sharing the heat of summer and sips of lemonade that his mother would bring out to them, Roy and his father grew close, and remained that way until his father's death later in life.

"Forty years is a while... my dad re-shingled his barn after twenty."

"Shingles usually last between twenty and thirty years." Roy paused to let out a short laugh. "I've been pushing it for ten. Really should have done it last summer when I first started seeing the leaks, but I hadn't the strength and was still too stubborn to accept your help around here."

"I imagine it's quite difficult to admit needing help. I don't envy growing old –no offense."

"None taken," Roy replied, glancing over his shoulder at the sound of a car coming up the driveway over the bridge. "I believe my grandchildren have arrived."

"I'll be on my way then; I don't want to keep you, and it seems to me we are done here."

"Thank you for the help today. I'll write your check, but first get the hay conveyor equipment put away. Just come inside the farmhouse when you're done."

Roy climbed down the ladder and Levi followed behind him. As Roy exited the barn doors, he could see his daughter faintly behind the reflection of the sun off the windshield of her silver

Prius. Love overcame him as he made eye contact with her. His daughter was the apple of his eye, and he felt she was the only thing he had done right in all the years of his life on earth. He'd never admit it to anyone out loud, but Tiff was his favorite child. She was the first-born and held a special place in his heart. The other kids gravitated more to their mother anyway; Tiffany and he were always close.

Parking in front of the garage that matched the paint of the barn, red with white trim, His daughter Tiffany stepped out of the driver side door and smiled at him. Hurrying her steps through the gravel, she ran up to her dad and hugged him as she let out what seemed to be a sigh of relief.

Watching over her shoulder as Jess got out of the car, Roy saw her slam the door. He suspected the drive hadn't gone that well for the three of them, but did the courtesy of asking without assuming. "How was the drive?"

"You don't want to ask..." she replied, glancing back at Jess as her daughter lingered near the corner of the garage.

Roy smiled. "I have a fresh batch of lemonade inside," he said, trying to lighten the tension he could sense. Seeing Henry was still in the backseat fiddling with something, Roy went over to one of the back doors and opened the door.

"Hi Grandpa," Henry said, looking up at him.

Leaning his head into the car, Roy smiled. "I'm looking for Henry, have you seen him? Because there's no way you are, Henry! He's just a little guy." Roy used his hand to show how tall Henry *should be* and continued, "About this tall, if my memory serves me correctly."

Henry laughed. "Stop Grandpa! It's me, I'm Henry!"

"I know... I'm just playing with you, kiddo! I haven't seen you in years! You've grown like a weed! Give your ol' Grandpa a hug!" Henry dropped his tablet on the seat and climbed over a suitcase of Jess's to embrace his grandpa in a warm hug.

"Can we go fishing Grandpa? Can we go today?"

Roy laughed as he stood upright. "Maybe tomorrow. The day is going to be over soon and I'd like to visit with your mother some."

Henry dipped his chin to his chest as he sighed. "Okay." Reaching into the back trunk area of the car, Henry grabbed his backpack and then scooted off his seat and out from the car. Just then, Jess let out a screech, which directed everyone's attention over to her at the garage.

"A mouse, are you kidding me?" With a look of disgust, she stomped off around Levi's truck, and down the sidewalk that led up to the farmhouse.

"Aren't you forgetting something?" Tiffany asked, which caused Jess to stop in her tracks. She turned around and put her hand over her brow to shield the sun.

"What, mom?"

"Your suitcases... maybe?" Tiffany replied with a sharp tone.

Roy placed a hand on Tiffany's shoulder. "That's okay. Henry and I can get them."

"No. Jess needs to get them." Roy could tell that his daughter was attempting to draw a line in the sand. A line that Roy and his late wife Lucille had drawn many times with her and the kids.

"Really, Mom?" Jess asked, placing a hand on her hip. "Those suitcases are heavy; the men should carry them. Grandpa is right."

Henry tugged on his mother's shirt corner. "I think you should let this one go, Mother." He smiled and nodded to Roy. "Grandpa and I have it."

Tiffany shook her head and turned away from Jess as she went to the back of the car. "She's so difficult, Dad. I hate it," Tiffany said, slapping the trunk. "She doesn't understand how life really works."

"Winnie," Roy replied. "Pick your battles."

The nickname *Winnie* came from when she was three years old. She would wake up in the middle of the night, push a chair up to the pantry and sneak the honey back into her bedroom. On several occasions, they would awaken the next day to find her snuggling an empty bottle of honey underneath her covers.

"I know. It's just hard sometimes, because everything is a battle with her lately."

Did you enjoy this preview?

*Pick up a copy of **The Perfect Cast** today!*

OTHER BOOKS

Diamond Lake Series

One Thursday Morning (Book 1)

One Friday Afternoon (Book 2)

One Saturday Evening (Book 3)

One Sunday Drive(Book 4)

One Saturday Evening

Embers & Ashes Series

Amongst the Flames (Book 1)

Out of the Ashes (Book 2)

Up in Smoke (Book 3)

After the Fire (Book 4)

Love's Enduring Promise Series

The Perfect Cast (Book 1)

Finding Love (Book 2)

Claire's Hope (Book 3)

Dylan's Faith (Book 4)

Stand Alones

Love Again

Love Interrupted

A Chance at Love

The Lost Truth

Visit www.tkchapin.com for all the latest releases

Subscribe to the Newsletter for special

Prices, free gifts and more!

www.tkchapin.com

ABOUT THE AUTHOR

T.K. CHAPIN writes Christian Romance books designed to inspire and tug on your heart strings. He believes that telling stories of faith, love and family help build the faith of Christians and help non-believers see how God can work in the life of believers. He gives all credit for his writing and storytelling ability to God. The majority of the novels take place in and around Spokane Washington, his hometown. Chapin makes his home in the Pacific Northwest and has the pleasure of raising his daughter with his beautiful wife Crystal. To find out more about T.K. Chapin or his books, visit his website at www.tkchapin.com.